tall, thin and BLONDE

Dyan Sheldon is the author of many books for young people, including *Confessions of a Teenage Drama Queen*; *And Baby Makes Two*; *The Crazy Things Girls Do for Love*; and *My Worst Best Friend*, as well as a number of stories for younger readers. American by birth, Dyan lives in North London.

Other books by Dyan Sheldon

tall, thin and BLONDE

Dyan Sheldon

WALKER
BOOKS

First published 1993 by Walker Books Ltd
87 Vauxhall Walk, London SE11 5HJ

This edition published 2012

2 4 6 8 10 9 7 5 3

Text © 1993 Dyan Sheldon
Cover photograph © Image source/Getty Images

This book has been typeset in Berkeley

Printed and bound in Great Britain by Clays Ltd, St Ives plc

British Library Cataloguing in Publication Data:
a catalogue record for this book is
available from the British Library

ISBN 978-1-84428-634-8

www.walker.co.uk

For M J K

Undressing in public

"**Look** at them!" I said to Amy. I gestured to a table at the other side of the café. A bunch of girls from our school were sitting together, drinking diet soda and shrieking. They all looked like Miss Perfect Teenager. You know the type. Size six and pretty, with a lot of make-up and too many teeth. We'd only been in high school for a few weeks, but I already recognised three of them. Two were cheerleaders. The other was Rosie Henley, one of the most popular girls in the entire school. Rosie Henley was tall, thin and blonde. She was so beautiful that it was hard to believe that she had ugly feet and hair on her toes like everybody else does. "They're so shallow and immature," I went on. "I bet all they ever talk about is boys and clothes."

This was the sort of statement that usually grabbed Amy's attention. Amy and I had always agreed on shallow, immature girls who never talked about anything but boys and clothes. Neither of us was ever going to be like that. Not even if we became stunningly gorgeous overnight. Not even if the cutest boy in the world asked us out. Not even if anyone asked us out. But this time Amy didn't even look up.

"I don't know if I'm going to have a burger today or not," Amy was saying. She scrunched up her nose, the way she does when she's thinking. "I don't really feel that hungry. Maybe I'll just have a salad plate."

"*A salad plate?*" I repeated. I looked over at her. Amy and I had been best friends since we were seven. In those seven years, the only time I remembered Amy saying she wasn't really hungry was just before she threw up at my tenth birthday party. "I don't think I want cake after all," she'd said. And then she'd clamped her hand over her mouth, jumped up from the table, ran into the kitchen and puked into the dog's bowl. Everyone but the dog and my mother had found it pretty funny.

Oh good grief, I thought. *Amy's going to be sick.* I looked over at Rosie Henley's table. *Right here in the middle of the Red Bay Mall. In front of girls who never even burp, never mind throw up.* I moved my bag out of her way. "What's the matter?" I asked nervously. "Don't you feel well?"

"I feel fine," said Amy, her eyes on her menu. "I'm just not very hungry, that's all."

"But we always get cheeseburgers," I protested. "It's our tradition."

All summer long, Amy and I had come to the mall every Saturday after swimming. We always had lunch at the Schooner Café, which was out in the open, in the centre of the main plaza, and had a fountain that looked like an old whaling schooner. We always sat at a corner table, because if you sat too close to the fountain you got wet. We always ordered the Whale of a Special – cheeseburgers, fries, onion rings, coleslaw and large sodas. After lunch, we'd walk around and check out the stores.

Amy made a face. "Oh, for God's sake, Jen." She sighed. "It's not like it's written in stone, is it? Amy Ford and Jenny Kaliski *have* to have a cheeseburger every Saturday or they'll turn into toads. I can have whatever I want."

"Well, of course you can," I said. I mean, what else could I say? It's not like I'm unreasonable or anything. It was just that Amy and I were so close that I guess I took it for granted that we always wanted the same things. And, besides, we'd had such a great summer hanging out together that I didn't want it to end. That was not only our first year in high school, it was the first year since third grade that we weren't in the same class. Amy was in Mrs

Gould's homeroom and I was in Mr Streb's. Which is like saying that Amy was in Florida and I was in Maine. We didn't even have the same lunch period.

I smiled at Amy. "What do I care what you have?" I asked. I sounded very reasonable. "Have two salad plates if you want. Have three! Have cottage cheese *and* tuna!"

While I was being reasonable, the waitress had come up beside us. She was very blonde and pretty, and only a couple of years older than we were. Amy turned to her with a smile. "I'll have the cottage cheese and a large diet Coke," she announced.

I couldn't believe my ears. Amy never drank diet soda. She and I had always agreed that ordering soda without sugar was like ordering a banana split and only getting a banana. It was what girls who were immature and shallow and only interested in boys and clothes drank! I had this sudden urge to throw my menu at her, but instead I politely handed it back to the waitress. "I'll have the Whale of a Special," I announced loudly. "With a root beer and a side order of fries."

The waitress looked at me as though I'd asked for a side order of grasshoppers. "You know it already comes with fries?"

"Yeah," I said. "I know it already comes with fries."

Amy turned to the waitress. For a second, I almost

thought she was giving the waitress a Look. A "the android's not with me" look. "You got that I want a *diet* soda, right?" asked Amy.

When the waitress left, I started teasing Amy. "Diet soda?" I joked. "You used to hate diet soda. You're not becoming shallow and immature, are you?"

Amy took a sip of her water. "There's nothing immature about caring about your appearance," she informed me coolly. "We're not children any more, you know. We have to watch ourselves."

Watch ourselves do what? I felt like saying. We'd never watched ourselves before, we'd always just *been*. But instead I changed the subject to geometry. Geometry was something I knew we agreed on. We talked about how much we hated geometry until our food came.

I was covering everything on my plate with ketchup when someone close by shrieked, "Amy!"

I looked up.

Amy tore herself away from the carrot curl she was trying to get on her fork and looked up too. She turned.

Rosie Henley and her friends were passing by our table on their way out of the café. They were carrying about a million shopping bags. Two of them – the two I didn't recognise – were smiling and waving at Amy like they were her long-lost sisters or something.

To my surprise, Amy smiled and waved back. I stared at her while ketchup plopped onto my food.

"Amy!"

"Kim! Amber!"

"Hi!"

"Hi!"

"What are *you* doing here?"

"What are *you* doing here?"

"We're shopping!"

"We're shopping, too!"

"See you in homeroom Monday!"

"See you Monday!"

Amy turned back to our table and her lunch. She looked happy.

I looked down at my burger. It had so much ketchup on it that it looked like a pizza. Pizza without cheese. "I didn't know you knew those girls," I said casually, scraping some of the ketchup to the side of my plate.

Amy bit into a stick of celery. "Well, now you do," she said.

Since I really didn't know what to say to that, I concentrated on eating my Whale of a Special. But I kept glancing over at Amy, nibbling her Rabbit Deluxe and sipping her diet Coke, and I started to think. Something was wrong. I don't know why I hadn't noticed before, but now that

I was thinking about it I realized that Amy hadn't been herself for at least a week. For instance, we always walked home together after school, and we always talked on the phone at least once a night. But Tuesday and Thursday I'd walked home alone, and Friday she hadn't been in when I'd called and she'd never phoned back. And as for today. . . Not only had Amy ordered a different meal and not told me about the new friends she'd made in homeroom, but she'd acted odd at swimming as well. Amy and I had joined the Red Bay Swimming Club the summer before. It was a serious training and competition club, and it was hard to get in and harder to stay. Amy and I were the only girls who hadn't dropped out after a month or two, and Amy was the club star. This morning, however, she'd done a couple of laps and then left the pool. "I just don't feel like swimming today," she'd said when I asked her why.

Thinking was making me lose my appetite. I pushed my half-eaten fries away.

Amy gazed at me over a forkful of cottage cheese. "Don't tell me you're full," she said in this sarcastic voice.

"I guess my eyes are bigger than my stomach," I answered.

She kind of smirked. "But they won't be for long if you keep eating like that."

* * *

After lunch, Amy and I strolled through the mall, like we always did. I began to feel a little better. Amy told me a funny story about some kid falling asleep in her French class while we checked out the music store and in the card shop we both bought this neat writing paper in neon colours. Maybe I'd just been imagining that Amy was acting odd. Everything seemed normal again.

We stepped off the escalator onto the second level of the mall. I pointed to the right. "How about going into Lost in Space?" I asked. Lost in Space was our favourite store. It only sold things that had to do with stars and planets and stuff like that. Lost in Space was where I bought the glow-in-the-dark galaxy I had on the ceiling of my room and my giant map of the sky. Ever since I was a little kid I'd been crazy about that sort of thing. Amy changed her mind from month to month about what she would do when she grew up, but I knew I was going to be an astrophysicist. It was all I'd ever wanted to be.

Amy shrugged. "I don't really feel like it today," she said.

I came to a stop. Amy kept going. The woman getting off the escalator behind us walked right into me. After I'd apologised, and the woman had apologised, and her little boy had pulled his lollipop off my jeans, I hurried to catch up with my best friend.

"What's with you today?" I demanded. "Have aliens

taken over your body or something? You don't seem to feel like anything you usually feel like."

She marched straight ahead. "Oh, give me a break, will you, Jen? I'm not a robot, you know. I don't have to do the same things over and over. Maybe I feel like doing something different today."

"Oh yeah?" I said. "Like what?"

She glanced over at me. "Like going to Miss America."

"Miss America?" I'd been right. Aliens *had* taken over Amy's body. Miss America was the trendiest store in the mall. We *never* went into Miss America. Girls who cared about nothing but boys and clothes and diet soda went to Miss America.

Amy nodded. "I want to get something for the dance next Saturday."

"The dance?"

She looked amazed. "Don't tell me you're not going!" cried Amy. As though either of us had ever been to a dance in her life. "It's the first big social event of the school year!"

"Me?" I stared into her eyes, half expecting them to light up and turn orange the way the eyes of people do whose bodies have been taken over by aliens. "Me, go to a dance?" Amy and I didn't go to dances. Dances were for girls who painted their toenails and wore perfume.

"Yes, *you*!" said Amy. She took hold of my arm and started steering me towards Miss America. "Jen," she said urgently, "we have to go. We're in high school now. We have to get into the swing of things or we'll never fit in."

Swing of things? Fit in? Was that a Michael Jackson CD playing in the background or the theme song from *The Twilight Zone*? "I don't know about this," I said as Amy pulled me through the doors of Miss America. It definitely *sounded* like Michael Jackson, but I looked around just in case gold-coloured aliens were standing in the shadows. "We never had to fit in before."

"That's because we were children before," said Amy. "Now we're young women. This could be the best time of our lives, Jen. You don't want to miss it, do you?"

Amy had once talked me into rubbing poison ivy all over myself because she'd said I was wrong and it was only milkweed. She'd once talked me into running away with her, and we'd spent an entire day in her grandmother's garage. She'd once talked me into painting my face with what had turned out to be indelible inks. And she'd been the one who'd said my father wouldn't care if we borrowed his bird-watching binoculars when we went to camp. That was the thing about Amy, she could always convince me in the end.

"Well, no," I said as she led me through sportswear to dresses. "I guess I don't."

The alien who had taken over the body of my best friend, Amy Ford, seemed to know her way around Miss America the way the real Amy knew her way around Jean Junction, where we usually bought our clothes. Jean Junction was a store. You know, it had racks of shirts and jeans, and on the walls it had signs: BOYS. GIRLS. LEVIS. WRANGLERS. LEE. SALE. The walls were white. It had fluorescent lighting.

Miss America was more like a disco. Not only did it have music, it didn't have fluorescent lighting. Instead, it had a few forty-watt bulbs pointed skyward, a lot of flickering coloured lights and hundreds of mirrors. Things dangled from the ceiling on wires. Everything was loud and shiny and packed together. It made me feel sort of dizzy. Or like I might break something. Or rip it by accident. Or touch it and get dirty. I began to wonder if maybe I should miss the best years of my life after all.

The alien who had taken over Amy's body wasn't as easygoing as the old Amy, either. She was very critical. She'd pull a dress from a rack, hold it up to herself in front of a mirror, move this way, move that way, squint, shake her head and put it back. "Too long," she'd say. "Too dark." "Too loose." She liked bright colours and short skirts. She liked lycra, lace and satin. She thought I should pin up my hair with a giant silver clip.

"Have you gone nuts?" I screeched.

She pulled my hair and stuck the clip on top. "It adds sparkle."

"Sparkle? Amy, I look like a Christmas ornament." An elf. An elf with tinsel on her head.

She shrugged. "OK, suit yourself." She tossed the clip aside and pulled something pink from a hanger and stuffed it into my hand. "But at least try this on."

I looked down at the thing in my hand. It could have been a dead flamingo. "Amy," I said, "I don't wear pink. I like green."

Any rolled her eyes. "No one's wearing green any more. And, besides, pink's your colour."

That was news to me. I hadn't worn pink since I was two years old and my hair had finally started to grow so people could tell I was a girl. I shook the thing in my hand. "What is it?" I asked.

She pointed to a mannequin who was sitting on a model motor cycle that was hanging from the ceiling. "It's that dress."

It was a *small* dead flamingo.

"But, Amy," I said. "Amy, I don't wear dresses." Especially not ones with less than a yard of material in them.

"Oh, for Pete's sakes, Jen. You can't go to the dance in your old jeans and a T-shirt. You have to wear a dress."

"But, Amy," I said. "I'm not – I don't go to dances."

The girl at the door to the dressing room handed Amy a ticket that said 3 and me a ticket that said 1.

"Everybody goes to dances in high school," said Amy. "Unless they're weird."

Weird? Amy and I had always prided ourselves on being unique. In seventh grade she never wore the laces in her sneakers and I always wore mismatched socks. In eighth, she had her hair spiked and I had three holes pierced in my right ear. But now we were in the ninth grade. Amy's hair had grown out and I'd gone back to wearing just one pair of earrings like everyone else. In ninth grade, apparently, we worried about being weird.

"This is our big chance to be popular," Amy went on, as though we'd been waiting for this chance for years. "It doesn't matter what happened before. It all starts now. You don't want to miss the boat, do you?"

I was going to ask her to explain exactly what she meant by "weird", but I couldn't. I couldn't because, all of a sudden, I was paralysed. Every cell in my body had turned to cement. Except the cells in my heart. The cells in my heart had turned to flowing molten lava.

My heart was going nuts.

I looked around. We were in a large bright room. It didn't have walls, it had mirrors. Mirrors in every direction. Giant spotlights shone down on us from overhead. Not only that, but this large bright room was filled with dozens of smiling and laughing Miss Perfect Teenagers. Most of them were in their underwear.

Amy went over to a mirror and put her dresses on a hook.

I managed to speak. "Amy," I whispered. "Amy, where are we?"

She was hanging up her jacket. "What do you mean, 'Where are we?'" She laughed, "We're in the dressing room, of course."

My blood began to flow again. I turned my head. "But it's open!" The dressing room in Jean Junction was divided into little cubicles, each with its own mirror and its own door. The doors all had locks.

Amy was kicking off her shoes. "Of course it's open."

I didn't wear pink, I didn't wear dresses, I didn't go to dances – and there was one other thing I didn't do. I didn't undress in public. Not ever. Except in gym, but I had figured out a way to get my gymsuit on under my regular clothes. It wasn't easy, but it worked. "Amy," I whispered, "Amy, I can't … I'm not … I—"

Amy reached out and yanked me next to her. She took the dead flamingo from my hands and put it on a hook. "Stop being such a baby," she ordered. "Nobody's looking at you. Just try on the dress."

I stared into the mirror. I could see half a dozen pretty teenage girls behind me stepping in and out of clothes. It was like being in an underwear ad. Not one of them looked embarrassed or self-conscious. Why should they? Not all of these pretty teenage girls were blonde, but it wasn't as if you'd really notice. They were all tall and slender. They all had small breasts and flat stomachs and tiny bottoms. Their small breasts and tiny bottoms were in grown-up-looking bras and panties in vibrant colours and attractive patterns.

But standing right in front of them in the reflection was a short, pudgy brunette. Her breasts were not small, her bottom was not tiny, and her stomach was not flat. She wasn't ugly, maybe, but she wasn't pretty either. Not like the other girls were. She was also not laughing and smiling like the other girls, who were happy to show off how perfect they were. She was rigid with terror.

Amy had taken off her shirt and was stepping out of her jeans. "Go on, Jen," she urged. "Try on the dress. I bet you'll look terrific."

I held up the flamingo. It was so skimpy that it must have starved to death. There was no way I was going to be able to pull it on over my jeans. "I don't think it's really me," I mumbled.

"Jen," said Amy, "just get undressed, OK? Stop acting like such a child. It's no big deal."

I glanced over at her. When had she gotten that shiny blue bra and bikini? What had happened to her hips? Why hadn't I ever realised before that Amy's hair wasn't really brown? It was dirty blonde. Much to my surprise, Amy looked just like all the other teenage girls in the room. Perfect. When has she stopped being just regular, like me?

I decided that what I could do was take off my T-Shirt, pull the dress over my head and then pull it down at the same time I was pulling my jeans off. Maybe if I was really fast, no one would notice that my mother still bought me white cotton bras – the kind that old ladies wear. Or that my underpants weren't bikinis. Only to be really fast, I'd need four hands: two to take off my T-shirt and hang it up, and two to pull the dress over my head at the same time.

Amy was shimmying into a slinky royal blue mini-skirt. "Gosh," she grinned, stopping in mid-shimmy to stare at my bra. "I didn't know they still made those things."

In the mirror, I could see the Miss Perfect Teenager behind me, a redhead in lacy purple underwear, smile. I dropped my T-shirt and started to tug on the dress.

"Uh, Jen," said Amy, her voice so loud she was practically shouting. "Jen, aren't you going to take off your jeans first? You don't want to stretch the dress, you know."

More than one Miss Perfect Teenager began to giggle.

"Oh, right," I mumbled. "Sure." I stopped yanking on the dress and started hopping out of my jeans. At least I hadn't put on my Garfield underpants that morning, I could be grateful for that. I caught sight of myself just before I banged into the mirror; my face was the same colour as the dress and my thighs were wobbling.

At last, I stood before the mirror in the outfit Amy said I was going to look terrific in. The mannequin had looked a lot different in that dress. The mannequin had looked sexy. I looked like a hot dog. A cocktail frank.

Amy was shaking her head. "I guess you were right." She sighed. "It isn't really you, is it?"

Someone in the corner laughed.

Life among the Martians

The last thing Amy said to me on Saturday afternoon was, "You'll think about going to the dance, won't you, Jen? It won't be the same if you don't go."

And I'd said, "Yeah, OK, I'll think about it."

I thought about it Saturday night while I watched TV. Should I go to the dance or should I stay home? Amy wanted me to go to the dance with her. I should go.

I thought about it Saturday night while I brushed my teeth. Dances and parties really weren't my scene. I felt uncomfortable in large groups of strangers. I felt uncomfortable when I wasn't wearing jeans. I'd never put on make-up in my life. The dressiest shoes I had were a pair of Hush Puppies. I couldn't go.

I thought about it while I flossed my teeth. If I did go, we'd hang out and have a good time. Together. Just like always. If I didn't go with her, would she go with her new friends, the Miss Perfect Teenagers who had been in the café? I should go.

I thought about it while I lay in the dark, staring up at the tiny glowing galaxy on my ceiling, feeling a little bit like a black hole. I'd never wanted to wear slinky dresses and fancy underwear and flirt and giggle like girls were supposed to. I wanted to have a planet named after me. I couldn't go.

I woke up thinking about it on Saturday morning. Maybe Amy was right. We weren't little kids any more. We were young women. We were in high school now, we ought to try different things. I should go.

I thought about it while I ate my father's special Sunday banana-nut pancakes. This was the first big social event of the year. It might change my whole life. It might affect my entire high school career. Especially if no one asked me to dance. Especially if I turned up looking like a cocktail frank. I couldn't go.

I thought about it while I helped my mother rake the lawn. Most girls my age had been on at least one date. If I never went to dances and things like that I might never have a date. Not ever. Forty-four and never been kissed. I should go.

I thought about it while I peeled the potatoes for supper. I'd have to wear my contacts if I went, not my glasses. But I hardly ever wore my contacts because I'd never gotten used to them. I shouldn't go.

I thought about it Sunday evening while I did my homework. Who knew, I might have fun at the dance. If I stayed home, on the other hand, I knew exactly how much fun I would have: a video, a bag of potato chips and a root beer's worth of fun. My mother said I looked really nice when I got dressed up. My father said I was cute. Maybe I should go.

I thought about it while I gave my dog, Percy, his weekly brushing. I couldn't go. I didn't have anything to wear.

I thought about it while I put out the garbage. I should go. "Nothing ventured, nothing gained," my mother always said.

My last thought as I fell asleep Sunday night was: *But I can't dance.*

So I was still thinking about it on Monday morning as I walked to meet Amy. Should I? Shouldn't I? I figured I'd discuss it with Amy on the way to school, but in the end I didn't. In the end, it slipped my mind.

Amy was waiting for me by the mailbox at the end of her road, just like always.

Well, almost like always. Even without my glasses on, I could see from down the street that she looked different. Taller. Older. Curlier.

I didn't pretend to hide my surprise. "What happened to you?"

Amy was smiling like one of those women in a TV commercial whose wash is so clean even her husband notices.

"What do you think?" She turned around a few times. "Do you like it? Do you think I look different? Do you think anybody will notice?"

Different? Would anyone notice? How could she ask? Percy might not have noticed, but anybody else who had ever seen her before would. Amy's hair, which was usually straight as a toothpick, was a mass of spirals.

"Did you just wake up like that this morning, or did you have it done?" I asked.

She shook her head so that the curls bounced. "I did it Saturday after I saw you." She spun around again. "Well … what do you think?"

"It looks great," I said. Which it did. It just didn't look like Amy. I glanced over at her as we started down Culvert Drive. "Did you have yourself stretched, too? You seem taller."

"It's the shoes," said Amy. She shook her head again.

I looked at her shoes. They were cowboy boots with heels. I was pretty sure Rosie Henley had a pair just like them. I wasn't going to ask Amy when she'd bought them, but I wondered. Saturday after she saw me? Or Sunday when she said she had to go somewhere with her parents? "It's not just the shoes." I looked at her more closely. She wasn't wearing ordinary jeans, like mine, but stretch ones. Tight black stretch jeans with her new top. What *had* happened to her hips?

"Amy," I asked, suddenly remembering the salad plate she'd had at the mall. "Amy, are you on a diet or something?" Amy and I had both made a solemn vow in sixth grade that we would never go on a date so long as we lived, unless we were really, really fat and it was affecting our health. We made this vow because of our mothers. Amy's mother mostly. My mother's always saying that she's going on a diet, but Amy's mother is always on one. It's an obsession. All she ever talks about is how fat she feels, and the only time she isn't on a diet is Christmas. She even keeps all the cookies and chips and stuff like that locked in the trunk of the car so she won't eat them. It's really hard to get a snack in that house.

Amy shook her curls and turned the corner. "No," she said, looking straight ahead. "No, I'm not on a diet. What makes you ask that?"

"You didn't eat much when we went shopping Saturday." I shrugged. "And I guess you look a little thinner."

"Really?" She was trying to sound like she didn't care,

but I could tell she was pleased. She shook her curls for about the hundredth time. "Well, maybe I have lost a few pounds since school started," she admitted. "I don't seem to have much appetite lately."

She'd had her appetite on Labour Day, though, when she'd beaten me in our annual How Much Stuff Can You Get on Your Hamburger Contest. "It must be high school," I said. "You know, because you're not a child anymore."

My sarcasm was wasted on her.

"I think you're right," said Amy, as we strolled up the walk to the main entrance. "Everything's changed now, hasn't it?" But before I could answer, she grabbed my arm and pointed towards the building. "Look," she ordered, already waving into the distance, "there's Kim and Amber."

I looked. Sure enough, there by the birch tree were Kim and Amber, looking perfect, and waving and sort of bouncing in place.

"I'm going to have to go, Jen," said Amy, suddenly sounding shy. "I promised Kim and Amber I'd meet them before the bell rang, so we'd have the chance to talk."

"Oh," I said. "Oh, sure."

"You understand, don't you? I mean, they are my friends too…" It was amazing how she could look at me and look at them at the same time.

"Oh, sure," I said. "Sure, I understand. I mean, I have new friends, too, you know. It's not like I have no one else to hang out with. I understand that you can't be with everybody at the same time. I know what it's like to—" I stopped talking when Amy was so far ahead of me that there was no way she could have heard what I said.

I stood at the end of the driveway by the EXIT sign, watching her run up to Amber and Kim, and thinking about how things had changed so suddenly. There'd never before been anyone Amy wanted to hang out with more than me.

It was a dull grey morning. Amy's red curls and her blue top stood out like the lights of a plane in a cloud. And Amber and Kim, bouncing and laughing, looked like the place the plane wanted to be. You know, the place where it was sunny and fun and everyone would have a good time. I shifted my books in my arms. And I was the cloud. Dark, damp and blowing apart. *Cut it out*, I told myself. *Stop making such a big deal out of it. It's not like it's the end of the world or something. So she has a couple of new friends? So what? So do you.*

I took a deep breath. I put a cheerful, pleasant expression on my face. I walked right into the EXIT sign. A bunch of boys coming up behind me started to laugh. I stood up as straight as I could, so I wouldn't look so short, and then I marched towards the building as though nothing had happened.

"It's a good thing she's not taller!" one of the boys shouted behind me. "She might have hurt herself."

"The nervous system, Mr Mackay? Is that what you said, the nervous system?" Mr Herrera, my biology teacher, was the only person I'd ever known who could sneer with his voice. He was sneering now.

Kevin Mackay, who sat in front of me, sort of shrunk down in his seat. "It isn't the nervous system?" He didn't so much ask it as gasp it.

Mr Herrera smiled the way a shark who was about to eat you might smile if sharks could smile. "No, Mr Mackay," sneered Mr Herrera, "It is not the nervous system. And if you had a brain in that skull of yours instead of wet newspapers, you wouldn't think it was." He folded his arms across his chest, looking around the rest of the class. "Everyone else knows the answer, Mr Mackay. Why don't you?"

"Endocrine," I whispered, hoping Mr Herrera wouldn't see my lips moving. Science had always been my favourite subject, but if I'd had Mr Herrera for my teacher for the last nine years it wouldn't have been. Mr Herrera didn't teach by making his subject exciting and interesting. He taught by terror. The only problem was that he was head of the whole science department. As much as I disliked him, I had to get along with him. I was in the honours programme, and as head of the department he also ran that.

Mr Herrera smiled a little harder. "Well, Mr Mackay. We're waiting."

It didn't seem biologically possible, but Kevin's neck was sweating. "Endocrine," I whispered again.

I could hear Kevin clear his throat and swallow. He'd finally heard me.

Unfortunately, so had Mr Herrera. "Miss Kaliski," he said in his slow drawl. "Miss Kaliski, when I need you to help me teach this class, I'll be sure to ask. For the present, however, I'd very much appreciate it if you'd keep your mouth shut unless actually asked a direct question."

I could feel my face turn red. The only good thing about Mr Herrera was that everyone was so afraid of him that no one even dared laugh. Still, I was pretty relieved that the bell rang just then.

Pretty relieved, but not completely relieved. I'd already made up my mind that I had to talk to Mr Herrera after class. The reason was that right before he had started tormenting Kevin he'd announced that we'd be dissecting frogs in a few weeks. He seemed to think this was some kind of treat. I didn't want to dissect a frog. I wasn't going to learn anything from it that I couldn't learn from looking at a picture in a textbook. All these frogs were being killed, and for no real purpose. Just so the boys could make disgusting jokes about frog intestines and the girls could complain about smelling like formaldehyde. Just so Mr Herrera could humiliate anyone who couldn't locate the pancreas of the common frog. I believed in scientific investigation, but I didn't believe in killing anything for no good reason, not even a frog. So I had to ask Mr Herrera to exempt me from the dissection. I'd watch, but I wouldn't take part. I sat at my desk, rationally and reasonably going over in my head what I was going to say, until everyone else had left the room. I didn't want an audience for this. Mr Herrera just loved having an audience.

"Mr Herrera," I said, getting to my feet just as he put his hand on the doorknob. "Mr Herrera, could I talk to you for one minute?"

I didn't hold out much hope that he would be very sympathetic to me, especially not after what happened with Kevin, but he was a man of science. He would listen to reason.

Or maybe he wouldn't.

Mr Herrera's eyes looked very cold behind his

steel-rimmed glasses as I made my request. "Squeamish, are we, Miss Kaliski?" he asked when I was done.

"No, Mr Herrera, it's not that I'm squeamish. It's a … it's a matter of principle."

"Oh, really? And what principle would that be?"

I explained again about not thinking the dissection was necessary to my knowledge of biology. I explained again that I was happy to watch, but I didn't want to be personally responsible for the needless death of a small amphibian.

"This is a frog we're talking about here," said Mr Herrera, "not the family dog."

"I know, but—"

Mr Herrera cut me off. "But nothing," he snapped. "I can't make exceptions, Miss Kaliski. You're in high school now."

My mother always says that I'm the most stubborn person she knows, next to my father. I tried again. "Excuse me, Mr Herrera," I said, "but I don't really think that's fair."

"Oh, don't you?" He looked at me as though I were something on a slide. An abnormal cell maybe. "Do me a favour, Miss Kaliski. Don't think, all right? Just do as you're told."

* * *

34

What I'd told Amy was true; I had made some new friends at Red Bay High. My new friends were Sue, who sat next to me in homeroom; Joan, who was in my math class; Marva, Joan's friend from middle school; Tanya, Sue's friend from for ever; and Maria, who had just moved to Red Bay and sat behind Tanya in history. They were all right. You know, they weren't Amy – actually, they were nothing like Amy. And they were definitely nothing like Amy's new friends. They weren't pretty or popular. Tanya looked a little like a football player, but none of them dated one. Their clothes weren't fashionable. They weren't particularly cool. But the biggest difference between Amy's friends and my friends was that practically everyone in the school wanted to be with Rosie Henley's crowd, but no one wanted to be seen with Joan, Tanya, Marva, Sue or Maria. As far as the in-crowd of Red Bay High was concerned, these girls were Martians. As far as I was concerned, they might be Martians but at least being with them meant I didn't have to eat lunch alone.

I hated eating lunch alone. The first week of school, I'd had no one to sit with, and I thought I was going to have to give up lunch for the rest of high school. I mean, what can you do? You just sit there staring at your plate or your sandwich bag, acting like you're not the only person in the whole world who has no one to sit with. You can try to read a book or pretend to study at the same time, but you always end up spilling stuff. I had mustard on my biology text, tomato seeds all over the first page of *Pride and Prejudice* and grease stains on my geometry notes from those first five days. And besides, everyone knows you're not sitting by yourself because you want to. I mean, even if you did want to, you wouldn't, would you? Because no one would think you were sitting alone by choice, they'd think you were sitting alone because you had dandruff or you smelled or nobody liked you. Even eating with Martians was better than that.

Everyone but Tanya was already sitting at a table at the back of the cafeteria when I got to lunch that Monday.

Maria smiled at me as I put my stuff down next to her. Maria dressed in second-hand clothes and was sort of mousy, but she looked really pretty when she smiled. "We thought you weren't coming," she said in her soft, almost apologetic way. "Sue wasn't sure if she saw you in homeroom or not."

Sue, I thought. *Sue probably wasn't sure that she was in homeroom.* I shook my head. "I had to talk to Mr Herrera after biology." I looked over at Sue. Everything about Sue was vague. Her hair was kind of brown, her eyes were kind of blue, her clothes never quite fit together, she never knew what day it was or what class she was supposed to be in. She was even eating her sandwich in a vague way, nibbling around the crust. "But I was sitting right next to you," I reminded her. "You were telling me about your neighbour's parrot."

Sue blinked. "Oh, right," she said. "I wasn't sure if that was today or yesterday."

Joan peered over her glasses at her. There was something in the way that Joan always peered over her glasses that reminded me of my mother. "Sue," said Joan, gently but firmly, "yesterday was Sunday." The way she said "yesterday was Sunday" reminded me of my mother, too. But her straight dark skirts and plain white blouses reminded me of my grandmother.

There was a blur of colour and the table shook. We all looked up. Tanya had arrived. I know I'm on the short side, but Tanya was the tallest girl I'd ever seen. She wasn't one of those tall skinny girls either. Tanya was *big*. The only boy in the whole school who was as broad and as tall as Tanya was Dwayne Miller, and he was a fullback.

"Hi there, campers." Tanya grinned. She was dressed in bright gold and green. In case you had trouble spotting her in a crowd. She pulled out the chair beside Marva and sort of threw herself into it. The table shook again. Tanya beside Marva was like daytime sitting next to night. Tanya always wore the brightest colours and was always loud and laughing, and Marva wore only purple or black and was moody and intense. "What's the good word?" boomed Tanya.

"Four more days till Friday," said Marva, not looking up from the book she was reading.

"But that's five words," said Sue.

Everyone ignored her.

I unwrapped my sandwich.

"Yuk," said Tanya. "What is this stuff?" She was staring at the lump of meat on her plate, scraping at the gravy with her fork. "It doesn't look as though it ever lived."

Marva made a face. "It probably never did," she said.

Joan caught my eye and groaned.

Marva's eye, shadowed in a colour called Midnight Plum, to match the streak in her hair, rose above her paperback. "Not unless you think being kept in a tiny box in the dark from the moment you're born, screaming in agony, is living," she said.

"Here we go," sighed Joan.

I gave silent thanks that I had a peanut butter and jelly sandwich today and not the cafeteria lunch.

"Are we talking about pork again?" asked Sue.

"We're talking about barbarians," said Marva, brushing some crumbs off the table. She reached into her lunch-box and took out a bowl of salad.

Tanya leaned her head closer to her tray. "What's that?" she asked, pretending that her lump of meat was talking to her. "It's not true what Marva says? You *were* happy? The one thing that you ever wanted in life was to be a chicken cutlet served with instant mashed potatoes and peas in the school cafeteria?"

"Oh, ha ha, very funny," said Marva. She waved her hand and the twenty-five bangle bracelets she wore went off like a car alarm. "You can joke all you want, Tanya, but it's not funny. Eating meat is really bad for you."

Tanya poked at the food on her plate again. "It wasn't so good for the chicken either." She winked.

Joan wodged her sandwich bag into a ball and threw it at Marva. "Marva, please," she begged. "Do you think we could have just one meal where we don't have to hear about our crimes against livestock?"

It wasn't that I didn't agree with Marva about battery chickens and stuff like that. I did. I wasn't a vegetarian, but I didn't think animals should be treated cruelly and have to suffer. It was another of my principles. Even I was pretty tired of Marva's lectures, though. "Yeah," I said, "let's talk about the dance." Since it was the only thing I'd been thinking about myself for two days, it was the only thing that came into my mind. Their reaction was a little different than Amy's would have been.

Five heads turned to me at once. Five voices spoke. "What dance?" they asked.

"Saturday?" I said. "The dance next Saturday? You know, it's the first big social event of the year."

Joan bit into a corn chip. "Oh, really?" she said.

"Well, whoopdeedoo," said Marva.

"I didn't know there was a dance," said Maria.

"I can't believe it!" cried Tanya. "A dance? Here at Red Bay High? And I haven't been asked to it yet?"

"Why did Mr Herrera keep you after class?" asked Sue.

I turned to her, a little surprised by her question. "What?" *How did we get from Saturday's dance to Mr Herrera?*

"Mr Herrera," Sue repeated. "You said you were late for lunch because he kept you late after class."

Tanya pretended to gag. "I didn't know you had Mr Herrera," she said. "Everybody says he's worse than the plague."

Marva broke a carrot stick in two. "They're wrong," she said. "He's worse than two plagues. My brother had him and he almost got him kicked out of school."

The rest of us all looked at one another. Everyone at Red Bay knew Marva's brother. He was a senior. And though he was really smart and everybody, even teachers, sort of respected him, he was even more eccentric than Marva was. Talk about weird!

"Why did your brother do that?" asked Sue.

Marva patted her shoulder. "No, Sue. Chris didn't try to get Mr Herrera kicked out. Mr Herrera tried to get Chris kicked out."

I decided to get back into the conversation. "He didn't make me stay late," I explained. "I just wanted to talk to him about something."

"What'd Chris do?" asked Tanya.

Marva opened a small jar and shook some sunflower seeds into her hand. "Who knows?" she shrugged. "Chris is always doing something."

Well that was true enough. Even I had heard how Chris County had led the protest against Styrofoam trays and cups in the cafeteria. You could see where Marva got it from.

"What about you?" asked Maria. "Was Mr Herrera nice to you?"

"For him he was. I mean, he didn't actually yell at me or anything." I'd finished my sandwich and potato chips and was starting my brownie. "I asked him if I could be excused from dissecting frogs."

"I have Mrs Ricco," said Sue. "Mrs Ricco doesn't believe in dissection."

"So do I," said Maria. "I don't know what I'd do if I had Mr Herrera. Jenny's right, he's always yelling."

"I have Mr Janover, and he doesn't believe in dissection either," said Tanya, "but it wouldn't bother me if he did."

Marva eyed Tanya's empty plate. "It couldn't if you could eat *that*," she said. Then she looked at me. "So," she said, "what did Herrera say?"

"He said he'd think about it." Which he had. *I'll think about it, Miss Kaliski*, he'd said. *But now, if you don't mind, I'd like to have my lunch.*

Marva took a container of fruit salad out of her lunchbox. "That means no," she informed me.

"Oh, you can't be sure" said Joan. "It could mean that he wants to think about it."

Marva jangled as she picked up her fork. "No, it doesn't," she said simply. "I know him. It means no."

Later, as we were getting ready to go to our next classes, I brought up the dance again. Subtly. Casually. "So," I said as we left the lunch room, "what about the dance? Are any of you interested in going?"

Joan shook her head.

Marva rolled her eyes.

"Not unless the Jolly Green Giant's going to be there to dance with me," laughed Tanya.

"What dance?" asked Sue.

Yes and no

On Tuesday night I had a dream. In the dream, I didn't go to the dance. Amy came over to show me how she looked in her blue mini and lacy blue top. She looked terrific. She was wearing big silver hoops in her ears and turquoise shadow on her eyes. She looked like a model. She looked grown-up. "I wish you'd change your mind," she said.

I was sitting on my old tricycle. My hair was in pigtails and I was wearing jeans and a flannel shirt. I rang the bell of the trike. "I'm not coming," I said. "I want to stay home and watch TV." I rang the bell again.

Amy disappeared. The next thing I knew, I was at the dance. I was standing on tiptoe at the window of the gym door. Inside it didn't look like the gym. It looked like a club. There were posters on all the walls and it was dark. There were purple spotlights everywhere and a real band. Everybody inside was smiling and laughing. It started to rain. I was in the hallway outside the gym, but I was getting wet. I tried the door. It was locked. Amy floated by in the arms of Dwayne Miller, Red Bay High's big football star. I banged on the glass. "Amy!" I shouted. "Amy! I've changed my mind! You were right! We're not little kids any more. I want to come to the dance after all. I want to be grown-up and popular too!" The storm increased. "Amy!" I screamed. "Amy! Let me in!" Everyone in the gym turned to look at me. They started laughing. Amy was laughing the loudest. "Amy!" I was practically crying. "Amy! Open the door!"

"I can't!" Amy laughed. The door disappeared. I was standing at the end of a dock. It was still pouring. The gym had turned into an enormous cruise ship. It was decorated with paper lanterns and coloured lights. The band were dressed like pirates. Amy was waving to me. "Goodbye, Jenny," she was calling. "Goodbye!"

"Wait!" I was yelling. "Wait for me! I don't want to be left behind! I want to come, too!"

Dwayne Miller suddenly appeared at her side. He put his arm around her. "It's too late, Jenny!" Amy laughed. "You've missed the boat!"

So that was why, on the way to school on Wednesday morning, I told Amy I'd decided to go to the dance.

"I knew you'd make the right decision," said Amy.

* * *

Mr Herrera, however, did not make the right decision. Mr Herrera said, "No." Science was supposed to be about logic and reason, but for Mr Herrera it was about rules.

"I can't make exceptions, Miss Kaliski," he informed me. "You're in high school now. You'll do what the rest of the class does or you'll get an F."

I didn't see Amy after school on Wednesday, but I phoned her that night. I had to tell someone, I was so outraged, and Amy was the person I always told everything to.

"Can you believe it?" I asked. "He's making me dissect a frog even though I'm not going to learn anything I couldn't learn from a textbook. Even though I'm not going to contribute anything to scientific knowledge."

Amy was filing her nails, I could hear her sawing away while she spoke. "I don't know why you always make such a big deal out of everything," she said. "Just tell him you'll dissect the stupid frog, and then when he isn't looking let one of the boys do it for you. It's what all the other girls do."

I tried to explain. "But, Amy, that's not the point. It's not that I *can't* do it, it's that I don't want to. It's a matter of principle."

"You can't fight city hall," said Amy. "And anyway,

what choice do you have? You might as well just go with the flow."

"It's just that I feel very strongly about this sort of issue." I raised my voice. "As a future scientist I am concerned with—"

"What you should be concerned with is what you're wearing Saturday," said Amy. "Have you given any thought to that, or have you been too busy worrying about reptiles?"

"Amphibians," I corrected. The truth was that I hadn't yet given any thought to what I was wearing because my argument with Mr Herrera had put the dance completely out of my mind.

Amy sighed. "Amphibians, reptiles … what's the difference? The dance is only three days away. Are you going to do anything to your hair?"

"To my hair?"

She sighed again. "And what about make-up?" she demanded. "Have you even thought about that?"

Why would I? The only time I paid attention to stuff like that was when I saw those posters about testing beauty products out on mice. "Well, no…" I said. "I—"

Amy huffed. "Really, Jenny," she said. "Sometimes I don't know what's going to happen to you. What would you do if I wasn't around?"

"I guess I'd stay home Saturday night," I joked.

Amy didn't laugh. "Why don't you come over after school tomorrow and we'll try out some make-up and hair styles and stuff."

We arranged to meet in front of the library after last period on Thursday. "Right after class?" said Amy. "Right after class," I said. So there I was, standing under my green umbrella outside the library, water beginning to seep through my sneakers, waiting for Amy. I looked at my watch again. Amy was late.

It was funny, but though I'd never thought much about my hair or make-up or anything like that before, as the afternoon went on I'd started to feel a little excited. What if Amy managed some incredible transformation? All through history I kept imagining what I might look like when Amy was through. Taller. Thinner. Prettier. Like a Before and After make-over in a magazine. I'd go into Amy's bedroom looking like one of those girls boys don't notice unless they want to borrow her maths homework; and I'd come out looking like one of those girls who never does her maths homework but whom every boy in her class wants to date. I wanted my watch again. I wished she'd hurry up.

My patience was beginning to wear out when the door opened behind me. I turned around, but it wasn't

Amy. I caught a glimpse of a long, hooded black cape, a pale thin face and black-ringed purple eyes. It was a vampire. The vampire's arms were filled with books. I turned back to the path.

The vampire stopped beside me. "Jen?" she asked, peering under my umbrella. "Jen, is that you?"

"Marva?" I should have known. Who else at Red Bay High would wear a cape instead of a raincoat? Especially one that was black on the outside and purple on the inside. Tanya, Joan, Maria and Sue might all be Martians, but Marva was the head Martian, there was no doubt about that.

"What are you doing out here in this deluge?" She laughed. "Waiting for the ark?"

"Not exactly," I said. "I'm waiting for my friend Amy."

Marva tucked her books under her cape. "That's not the blonde, is it? The one with the perm I sometimes see you with in the mornings?"

I nodded. "Yeah," I said, "that's Amy."

"She's gone," said Marva.

"Who's gone?"

"Your friend Amy. She's in the same class as me last period. I saw her leave right after English."

"Are you sure?"

Marva nodded. "Sure I'm sure. There were a couple

of girls waiting for her in the hall, and they were talking about not being late for something."

All of a sudden I felt as though I'd been waiting for my friend Amy for a very long time. My feet were soaking. The bottoms of my jeans were wet. My arm hurt from holding the umbrella. *How could she go off and leave me like this?* I forced myself to smile. "I guess I must have mixed up the days," I said. "She must have meant tomorrow."

"You live past Burr, don't you?" asked Marva.

I nodded. Numbly.

"I go that way, too," she continued. "You want to walk together?"

For a second I just stared at her. I had this sudden image of the two of us on our way home, me looking like a green mushroom with feet, and Marva looking like Countess Dracula. What if someone saw us? Then I had another sudden image, this one of Amy going off with Amber and Kim. "Sure," I said. "You want to hold the umbrella?"

"So what'd Herrera decide?" asked Marva as we walked past the teacher's parking lot. "Is he going to exempt you from the frog carving?"

I told her what he'd said.

"What did I tell you?" asked Marva. "When Herrera says he wants to think about something he means 'no way, not in a million years'. It's because he doesn't think, he just does what he's always done."

"I can't believe it," I said for about the hundredth time since the day before. I kicked a stone and it splashed into a puddle. There was a rumble of thunder in the distance. "No one else in the whole world makes this stuff mandatory any more."

"It's because you're in advanced biology," said Marva.

"But it's not like I want to be a doctor," I complained. "I want to be an astrophysicist. A first-hand look at the intestines of a frog isn't really important to me."

"It doesn't matter," said Marva. "It's exactly what happened to Chris."

"Chris?"

"My brother."

"Oh, right," I said. "Chris."

"He was the best student in the class, so there was no way Herrera was going to let Chris bend the rules. He said he would set a bad example. I've never seen Chris so mad. He hates inflexibility. And when Herrera tried to have him suspended…" She rolled her eyes. "Chris swore he'd get even before he graduated, or die in the attempt." We turned a corner.

"So what are you going to do now?" Marva wanted to know as we walked up her block.

"Now?" What was she talking about? "What do you think I'm going to do now? I'm going home."

Marva made a face. "No." She moaned. "About Herrera."

"What can I do?" I asked. "I'm going to cut this poor little frog open and then I'm going to go home and feel guilty about it for the rest of my life."

We came to a stop in front of a big old house that looked like it might be haunted. Marva didn't have to say anything, I knew it must be hers. My family lived in a small ranch house. Our house was white with dark green trim. Marva's house was blue. The paint was peeling in places, but it was definitely blue. Bright blue. The trim was pink. I'd never seen a house that shade of blue before. In fact, I'd never seen anything that shade of blue before. There seemed to be a lot of stuff on the front porch. I half expected to see Boris Karloff appear among the old furniture and refrigerators, laughing his evil laugh. If Marva was the head Martian, then this was Martian Control.

A sudden flash of lightning lit up the sky. I think I might have screamed, but my attention was caught by something on the roof. Right where the attic window should have been there was this odd-looking wooden box. "What is that, Marva?" I asked, pointing. "Is it some kind of bird house?"

Marva didn't even look up. "It's not a bird house, it's my brother's bat roost." She said it as though everybody had a bat roost on their house. Maybe Marva really was Countess Dracula.

I squinted into the rain, looking to see if there were any bats circling the chimney.

Marva put a hand on my shoulder. "You know, Jen," she went on, undaunted by the fact that I had changed the subject, "you don't have to dissect this frog, no matter what Mr Herrera says. You do have options."

Options? "I do?" I tore my attention away from the bat roost.

She nodded. "Sure you do. For instance, you could just miss that class."

"You mean *cut* it?"

She waved one hand dismissively, bracelets jangling. "No, of course not," said Marva. "Not cut it exactly. I mean wake up with a really bad headache that morning."

Oh, no, not cut the class, just wake up with a headache. "I couldn't do that," I said. "First of all, it's going to take up at least two or three lab periods. I'd have to get more than a headache to miss it. Pneumonia, maybe. And second of all," I explained, "if I don't do the frog, Mr Herrera will give me an F."

Marva didn't blink. "So?"

"So?" I echoed. "So science is what I'm interested in. I can't afford not to do well in biology."

"Go to Mrs Loomis then," suggested Marva. "File a formal complaint."

Mrs Loomis was our principal. Everyone called her The Terminator. I'd rather dissect a live iguana than complain to her about Mr Herrera. Where *did* Marva get these ideas?

"That's what Chris did."

Oh, Chris. That was where Marva got those ideas, I should have known.

"And what happened?" I asked. "Did it help?"

Marva shrugged. "Not exactly. But Chris probably went a little over the top, as usual. He was *very* upset. I think he told Mrs Loomis that Mr Herrera would have made a good KGB agent. He may have even said that Mr Herrera would have been better off working in the Spanish Inquisition than in a high school science department." She gave me an encouraging smile. "But you're not as temperamental as Chris. I'm sure she'd listen to you."

"I'll think about it," I promised. Meaning no. I looked at my watch. "Good grief," I said, "is that the time? I'd better get going. I have to fix supper for my parents."

"I'll tell you what," Marva said as she handed me back the umbrella. "I'll ask my brother what he thinks you should do. He's always full of ideas."

I looked over at the bright blue house with the bat roost attached to it. "Terrific," I said. "I feel better already."

I let myself into my house through the kitchen. Neither of my parents was home from work yet. I kicked off my sneakers and left them by the door. I hung up my jacket so it would dry, put my umbrella in the sink and threw my things down. The sound of my boots hitting the table woke up Percy. He leapt off the couch (where he wasn't allowed to sleep) and came racing in to say hello. He jumped into my arms. He's not supposed to jump into my arms either, because he's too big really, but he does it anyway. I kissed the top of his head and told him he was a good boy, and then I put him down. I looked at the clock on the wall. I had at least an hour before I had to start supper. Time for a snack before Percy's walk.

I had just sat down with a glass of juice, a bowl of corn chips and Percy when the phone rang. It was Amy. To tell you the truth, I'd completely forgotten about her during my walk home with Marva. But the second I heard her voice, I remembered. And I remembered how annoyed I was. "Oh, it's you," I said. "I thought maybe you had amnesia."

Amy laughed. "I did. I had temporary amnesia."

I chewed on a couple of chips. Loudly. But I didn't say anything. I didn't want to give in too easily.

"I'm sorry, Jen," Amy apologized. "I really am." She did sound sorry.

"I stood in the rain for hours," I complained. "I couldn't believe you didn't come."

"Jen, I'm really and truly sorry. What more can I say? I didn't do it on purpose, you know."

I could feel myself weakening. "You were going to do something with my eyes," I reminded her. "*And* my hair. Now what I am going to do about the dance?"

"I'll make it up to you, Jen. You can come over early on Saturday and we'll do it then."

I weakened some more. "Well, I guess we could do it Saturday," I said slowly. "If I have the time." I tossed a few more chips into my mouth and crunched. She sounded sorry, but I didn't want to completely forgive her until I'd heard her excuse. "So where were you?"

She stopped sounding sorry. "It was the cheerleading try-outs today," she said quickly. She sounded excited. "And in all the rush and everything I forgot I was supposed to meet you."

I stopped chewing. I swallowed. This wasn't the excuse I'd expected. "I didn't know you were going out for the cheerleaders," I said. I knew how I sounded. I sounded amazed. When we were in third grade, Amy used to fool around playing football. I always wanted to be the referee and Amy always wanted to be fullback. Neither of us had ever wanted to be a cheerleader. "You're my best friend," I said. "I can't believe you went out for cheerleaders and you didn't say one word to me." I sounded amazed and hurt.

"Well," she said slowly, "I wasn't going to. I mean, you know, I've never really been the cheerleader type, but everyone convinced me that I was a natural. So at the last minute I decided to give it a try." She laughed. "Nothing ventured nothing gained, right?"

I didn't need to ask who everybody was. Everybody must be Kim and Amber. "And are you a natural?" I asked.

The excitement came back in her voice. "Well, yes," she said, "I guess I am. I made the squad."

My best friend not only had curly hair and no hips, my best friend was a cheerleader. Things were changing a little fast for me. "Well, congratulations," I said. I had to say something. "That's great."

"Thanks," said Amy. "I knew you'd be pleased."

How had she known I'd be pleased? I looked at the bowl of corn chips. I smiled. I didn't feel pleased. I felt that if that bowl of corn chips had been a bug, I would have stepped on it. "Yeah," I said. "I'm thrilled."

No tutu for you

Probably the best thing about the Saturday dance was that worrying about it took my mind off other things, like frogs and cheerleaders.

Not that I wanted to worry about it. I didn't. I didn't even want to think about it. It wasn't important, I kept telling myself. It was stupid to spend so much time trying to decide what shoes you were going to wear or whether or not you should wear a skirt. It was a waste of time and energy. But I worried anyway. I worried Thursday night. I worried all day Friday.

What should I wear? What would everyone else be wearing? What if Amy's make-over didn't work? What if I looked the same After as I did Before? Should we get there on time? Or should we get there late? What would I do when someone asked me to dance? Were you supposed to talk while you danced? Or were you supposed to dance and talk later? Not that it really mattered, of course, because I couldn't dance. Not socially. I used to be into ballet, when I was younger, but it wasn't the same thing. And even if I could dance, which I couldn't, no one was going to ask me to dance. Which brought me to another problem. What did you do when you weren't dancing? Did you just stand there, or would there be someplace to sit down? Would the people who weren't dancing talk to one another, or what? And then a really awesome thought hit me. What if some geek asked me to dance? Then what would I do? How could you tell someone that you didn't want to dance with him without letting him know that you didn't want to dance with him not because you didn't feel like dancing, but because you'd rather have your teeth drilled than dance with him? Would there be refreshments?

Saturday was worse.

It took me five hours to get dressed for the dance, not counting the two showers and the bath I took.

The main problem was that I really did have nothing to wear. Most of my jeans were baggy and most of my shirts were flannel. You know, great for camping in the wilderness, but not exactly right for the first big dance of the year. I had a few dresses and skirts and blouses at the back of my closet, but they were mainly things my grandmother and my mother had given me for presents.

Amy, Kim and Amber wouldn't have been caught dead in any of them.

On the other hand, it was just as well that I had so little choice. Because my second problem was that I couldn't make up my mind. I'd try something on. Then I'd go into my parents' room to see how it looked in my mother's full-length mirror. Then I'd go into the kitchen, where my mother was fixing the washing machine, and I'd ask her what she thought. Then I'd go back in the bedroom for a second look. Then I'd try on something else.

It was the first time I realized how unreliable mothers are as judges of fashion. No matter what I put on, my mother said it looked nice. She didn't care if it was green or had bows on or made me look like Miss Piggy. "That looks lovely, dear," she said. Unless it was something that was almost passable. Then she'd say, "Honey, don't you think it's a little ... um ... short?"

The only thing my father said to me all afternoon was, "Jenny, you aren't still in the bathroom, are you?"

Finally, just when I was about to start crying, my mother threw down her wrench and rushed me to the mall. She helped me pick out a stretchy black skirt and a deep yellow top. My mother and the salesperson said the yellow brought out the rich brown colour of my hair and my eyes. When I was all dressed, I went to show my parents.

"Really, honey," said my mother, "you look great."

My father said, "Isn't that skirt a little short?"

"That's the way they're wearing them now," said my mother.

When I got to Amy's, the first thing she said to me was "Hi! Isn't this going to be great?" She was wearing her new blue skirt and a pale pink silk shirt. She looked like a model. An eighteen-year-old model. For some reason, I started to feel short and chubby and not much more than twelve.

The second thing she said was, "Do you want to change into your clothes for the dance after I make you up or before?"

"This is what I am wearing to the dance," I said.

"Oh," said Amy. "Oh, of course." She smiled as though she'd been kidding, but I could see in her eyes that she'd been perfectly serious.

"What's wrong with it?" I asked. I glanced at myself in the mirror. "Does it make me look fat or something?"

Amy shook her head. "No, no, it doesn't make you look fat..." She drew her eyebrows together in that way she has. I could tell she was debating whether or not she should tell me the truth.

"What is it?" I pushed. "Is it too long?"

"No," said Amy, "it's not too long." She was chewing thoughtfully on the end of a strand of her hair. "It's just that no one's wearing those black skirts any more," she said at last.

I looked down. "They're not?" Why hadn't anyone told me? Or the saleslady? And why were they allowed to continue selling them if no one was wearing them? "Well, there's not much I can do about that now," I said. I looked at Amy. Her eyebrows were still drawn together. "What?" I asked.

She looked pained. "It's the top," she said slowly. "It's not really your colour."

"It isn't? You don't think it brings out the rich brown colour of my hair and eyes?"

"I think it makes you look like a plague victim." She laughed so I'd know she was making a joke.

"Ha ha," I said.

"Maybe you can wear something of mine," Amy suggested. She frowned. Her eyes went from my head to my feet. I looked down. But I didn't get as far as my feet. All I saw were my knees. They were white and pudgy. They looked like un-iced cupcakes. My father had been right. The skirt was too short.

Amy wasn't too impressed with what she saw either. "I must have *something* that would fit you," she sighed.

Oh, sure, I thought, *like a cardboard box or a garbage bag, something like that.*

"You don't have to go to any trouble," I assured her, wishing I had worn jeans after all. Jeans and stilts. "I'm OK wearing what I have on."

She didn't say anything, but she gave me this look. *That's what you think*, said her look. She smiled bravely. "If only you were an inch or two taller," she said. "Or a little … you know … smaller…"

"Or someone else," I suggested.

Amy gave me a wink. "That would help, too," she said with a laugh.

She stopped laughing when she tried to do something with my hair. "You should curl it," said Amy, rubbing gel into it to "give it some body". "Nobody wears their hair like this any more. It went out with bell-bottoms."

I winced as she rubbed a little too vigorously. "But I don't want it curled," I protested. "I like it straight."

She gave me a slightly pitying look. "It's too bad it's so dark," she said. "You can't even have it lightened."

"Maybe I should just wear a wig."

"It works for Beyonce," said Amy.

Amy wasn't laughing while she made me up, either. "Stop blinking, Jen," she ordered. "How can I do your eyes if you keep blinking?"

"I can't help it. It's a reflex action. That's how your eye protects itself from foreign objects."

"There's nothing foreign about eyeliner and mascara," said Amy.

I didn't exactly agree with that. "I feel like my lashes are glued together."

Amy stepped back. She put her head to one side and pursed her lips. She looked like an artist deciding whether or not she had gotten the blue right in the sky.

"Well?" I asked. She'd put so much lipstick on my mouth that my lips made a noise when I moved them.

"Not bad," said Amy. She passed me the hand mirror. "See for yourself."

I stared at myself in the glass. My hair seemed to have been electrocuted, my skin was an unnatural shade of pink, my eyelids were an unnatural shade of blue, and my mouth looked as though I'd been sucking blood.

"Well?" asked Amy.

I couldn't answer. If this were After, you had to wonder After what?

We weren't at the dance for more than three minutes before I began to wish that I really were someone else. Someone who lived in Alaska or Iceland. You know, a place where it was cold and dark a lot and they didn't have many dances. Someone whose best friend had found her something else to wear instead of the short black skirt and yellow top her mother had told her she looked so nice in.

We walked through the door. "Gee, doesn't it look great?" asked Amy.

It was nothing like my dream. It looked like the gym decorated with balloons and streamers. Instead of a live band there was a DJ. The DJ was Mr Mantin, the music teacher.

She looked around the room. I looked around the room, too. There were a few couples dancing, but mostly kids were just standing around in groups, boys in one huddle and girls in another. I didn't see anyone I knew. Not to talk to, anyway.

But Amy did.

"Look!" she squealed. "Look! There's Amber and Kim and Samantha Wister, the co-captain of the cheerleaders." She jabbed me in the ribs. "And look!" she breathed. "There's Rosie Henley!" Except for Rosie Henley, they were all waving at her. Rosie Henley was too cool to wave. She just smiled like a queen greeting a peasant.

Amy grabbed my arm. "We'd better go over and say hello," she said.

"What?" I don't know why, but I wasn't prepared for this. I'd thought Amy and I were going to hang out at the dance together. By ourselves.

She waved back. "They're waiting," she hissed. "We can't just stand here…"

"But, Amy—" I began. She was already walking away. I pulled myself up to my full height, and I strode after her. I might not be part of her new crowd, but I wasn't going to stand there all alone.

They were all happy to see one another. They hugged each other. They started talking and giggling. I smiled. Amy told each of them how great she looked. She loved Rosie's hair. She loved Samantha's earrings. She loved Amber's dress. She couldn't get over Kim's new shoes. They told Amy how great she looked. Samantha loved Amy's skirt. Kim loved the way she'd done her eyes. Rosie used to have a blouse in exactly that shade of blue.

No one said anything to me. I just stood there, smiling. I could feel my skirt shrinking and my knees swelling. I was getting shorter. I glanced at my watch. Why hadn't I ever realized before how hairy my arms were? I looked like a jungle girl. I clasped my hands behind my back. Amy said something that made everyone laugh. I smiled harder. And then I remembered that we'd had spaghetti for supper. My mother always put garlic in her spaghetti sauce. And I'd eaten it! I'd eaten garlic before the dance! I stopped smiling and clamped my mouth shut. My feet began to sweat. Good grief, that was all I needed.

I lowered my head a little to see if I could smell anything. My contact fell out. I didn't usually wear them, because they never really fit right, but Amy had convinced me that I couldn't go to the dance in glasses.

These things don't happen in real life, I told myself. *They only happen in the movies.* As casually as I could, I got on my knees. Someone – Amber, I think – wanted to know what I was doing. "Listening for buffalo," I said.

I knew they were exchanging looks above my head. Someone – Samantha, I think – said, "Was that a joke?"

Amy giggled nervously. "Jenny has a very unusual sense of humour."

"She certainly has a very unusual sense of something," said Rosie Henley.

"Maybe that's the way they dance on her planet," said Kim.

"I wouldn't crawl around in that outfit if I were her," said Amber.

Amy stepped forward. I held my breath, expecting to hear the unforgettable sound of a plastic lens being ground into the floor of the gym by size five pumps in a vibrant shade of blue.

"Don't move!" I shouted. "I've lost my contact."

Amy laughed. "Oh, your *contact*." She moved and my heart stopped. "Jenny lost her contact," she told them.

She sounded relieved. "Why didn't you say you lost your contact?"

"Because she was too busy listening for buffalo," said Samantha.

When I came back from the girls' room after putting my contact back in, everyone was gone.

I sat down on the bleachers to wait for them to come back. I figured they'd gone somewhere to smooth down their eyebrows or something. I waited.

Slowly, I began to notice that I was the only person in the entire gym who was by herself. Even the people you knew no one would ever dance with were with other people no one would ever dance with. I scanned the crowd, hoping the Martians might have shown up after all. I suddenly had a real longing to hear Tanya's too-loud laugh, or see Sue standing in the doorway with that "What Am I?" expression on her face. Even Marva in her Countess Dracula cape would have been a relief. But they weren't there. I waited some more.

I began to feel really self-conscious, Whenever someone looked my way, I could hear them thinking, *Good grief! Look at her clothes! Doesn't she know that black is out? Doesn't she know that yellow makes her look ill? How could she dare to show those knees? Look at how short and chubby she is! Hasn't she ever heard of self-improvement?* I waited some more.

Eventually, I spotted Kim, Amber, Amy, Samantha and a couple of boys who were on the football team, talking at the other side of the room. Dawyne Miller was standing next to Amy, smiling. Sort of like in my dream. I continued to wait.

Amy started dancing with Dwayne Miller. He was still smiling. There was a group of girls sitting at the other end of the bleachers. They looked at me and I looked at them. I turned away. They started laughing.

Up until this evening, the worst moment of my life had been when I was nine years old. Back then, I spent my Saturday mornings not at swimming club, but at Miss Marilu's Academy of Dance. I was in the advanced ballet class. There were twelve of us in the advanced class. Eleven of us were tall and slender, and called "my little swans" by Miss Marilu; the twelfth one was me. Miss Marilu called me Jenny. I loved ballet. All year long, I looked forward to the big end-of-year recital, when we got to wear these beautiful costumes and dance on stage. Back then, I liked having the spotlight on me. The year I was nine, Miss Marilu choreographed the ballet herself. It was about a fairy princess and a frog. The princess and her friends got to wear pink tutus and tiny silver crowns on their heads. The princess's tutu was sprinkled with stars. The frog and his friends wore green leotards and hoods so you couldn't see their ears. All the frog had to do was leap around and make sure the princess didn't fall on her face, but the princess was the star. I wanted to be the princess. I had my heart set on it. I was one of the very best dancers in the class, so I knew that I had a chance. I practised for weeks. I twirled through the kitchen. I leapt across the living room. I spent hours in the bathroom, using the towel rack as my *barre*. I stood in front of the mirror at the back of my mother's closet, picturing myself in the princess's tutu.

At last, the day of the audition arrived. Louise Leftbridge was out with the flu. Arabelle Mulson forgot the routine. Pamela Hindrikson stumbled twice. But I was terrific. I was flawless. I was the princess down to the tips of my toes. Even Miss Marilu praised me. "Excellent, my dear," said Miss Marilu. "Very, very good, indeed." She shook her head. "It's amazing," said Miss Marilu, "but you really have a talent." You'd have thought she'd just discovered that I could fly. Flushed with pleasure, I sat down to wait for Miss Marilu to assign the roles. Everyone agreed that I was a sure thing for the princess. I was so excited I could barely sit still.

Miss Marilu made me the frog. "But I want to be the

princess," I protested. "I've been practising for weeks." Miss Marilu smiled at me kindly. She patted my shoulder. "I'm afraid that you're not really built for the role of the princess," said Miss Marilu. She patted my shoulder again. I wasn't quite sure what she meant. She explained. "The princess must be slender and graceful," said Miss Marilu. She gave me another kind smile. "There will be no pink tutu for you," Miss Marilu bellowed. "But you will make a most excellent frog." I burst into tears.

If I'd still been a child and not a young woman in high school, I might have burst into tears while I was sitting by myself on the bleachers, watching everyone else have a wonderful time. Watching Amy laughing and tossing her curly blonde hair while she danced with Dwayne and didn't once look in my direction.

But I wasn't a child and I was in high school, so as calmly and casually as I could I stood up. I walked slowly towards the door. I crossed the hallway. I entered the girls' room. There were a few girls brushing their hair and studying their faces in the mirrors over the sinks. I strolled to the corner booth. I locked it behind me. I looked at my watch. It was nine twenty-five. The dance wasn't over till eleven, when my father would be picking us up. I couldn't walk home, because it was too late. I sat down to wait. Now that I knew what you did if you weren't dancing, I vowed that if I ever went to a dance again I'd be sure to bring a book along.

When the dance was finally over, I went back into the gym and signalled Amy that I'd meet her outside. She was talking and laughing with Dwayne, Kim, Amber and a bunch of kids I didn't know. She nodded briefly in my direction. When my father came I got into the front seat and Amy got into the back. My father asked us if we'd had a nice time. I said, "Uh huh." Amy spent the ride home telling my father about the nice time she'd had, blah-blah-blah. My father spent the ride home nodding and pretending to be interested. I spent the ride home changing the station on the radio.

"So," said my father as we watched Amy let herself into her house. "Your very first high school dance. I'm glad you girls had such a good time."

I swallowed hard. "Yeah," I said. "So am I."

Who will tell you the truth if your best friend won't?

I cried for a few hours when I got home on Saturday night, and then I decided that the quickest way to forget about the dance was to act as though it had never happened. People do that sort of thing all the time. My Uncle Jim was in Vietnam but he never talks about it. Anytime someone even mentions the word "war" Uncle Jim gets this blank look on his face and walks out of the room.

That's what I would do. Anytime anyone even mentioned the word "dance" I'd get this blank look on my face and walk out of the room. I wasn't going to re-live every gruesome moment of sitting on the bleachers by myself, feeling as though there were a spotlight on me. I wasn't going to keep remembering the hours I spent in the girls' room, reading the graffiti over and over, even though there was one limerick about Mrs Loomis and Arnold Schwarzenegger that I couldn't get out of my head. I was going to act as though there'd never been a dance.

When I came down to breakfast Sunday morning and my mother asked me if I'd had a nice time I said, "Yes," and then asked her some questions about her compost heap. My mother loves to talk about her compost heap. I spent most of the day doing my homework and reading a really great book about the cosmos that the town librarian recommended, which cheered me up a lot. I was a little worried that Amy might bring up the dance when I saw her Monday morning, but I didn't see Amy Monday morning because Kim's mother gave her a lift to school.

By lunch on Monday I was feeling almost normal. I even managed to cross the cafeteria without thinking that everyone was looking at me and whispering, "Isn't that the girl who spent the dance in the toilet?"

I spotted the Martians at the back of the room. Not that it was difficult. There was no mistaking Marva, wearing nothing but black, including her lipstick, or Tanya in the brightest orange overalls I'd ever seen. Marva looked like Morticia, and Tanya looked like a giant pumpkin. I started to smile. It surprised me to realise that I was kind of glad to see them.

Joan looked up as I sat down beside them. "So how was the dance?" she asked. I tried to look blank. "What?" I couldn't believe it. It hadn't even occurred to me that the Martians would remember the dance.

Maria leaned across the table towards me. "Oh the dance!" she said with a sigh. "I was thinking about you all weekend."

She was? Thinking about *me*?

Apparently, she was. "What did you wear?" she wanted to know. "Did you meet anyone nice?"

Marva saved me from having to answer. "You've got to be kidding." She hooted, bangles clanking. "Who would she ever meet at a dance at this school? Some dumb football player with an ego as big as a stadium?"

Sue stopped mid-bite. She gazed at me musingly, tomato and lettuce falling out of her sandwich. "You went to a football game?" she asked.

I started taking things out of my lunch-box, slowly and methodically. I was still trying to look blank.

Tanya blew a straw wrapper across the table at Sue, but it was to Marva she spoke. "Don't be so prejudiced," she ordered. "My cousin's a football player and he happens to be a great guy. *And* very smart."

Marva made a face. "Are you sure he's *your* cousin?" she teased.

Sue gave me this big smile of understanding. "Oh," she said. "You went to the dance with Tanya's cousin."

Looking blank was easy as along as I talked only to Sue.

Joan peered at me over her glasses. "So come on, Jenny," she coaxed. "What was it like?"

Maria nodded . "You have to tell us every detail," she said. "None of us are ever going to go to a dance, that's for sure."

"None of us would want to go to one," said Marva.

"Speak for yourself," said Tanya. She started bopping in her seat. "I for one happen to be a great dancer. They clear the floor when I get up to dance."

"They'd have to," said Marva. "No one would want you to fall on them."

"Would you two give Jenny a chance to talk?" Joan nudged me. "So?" she persisted. "What was it like?"

I unwrapped my sandwich and just looked at it for a second. I raised my head. The five of them were staring at me expectantly. I stared back blankly. *Just tell them you had a nice time*, I told myself. *That's all they want to hear.*

"It was hell," I said. "It was the school dance from hell."

So, even though I hadn't planned to, I told the Martians all about Saturday night. In detail. I told them about how Amy had made me look and how her friends wouldn't talk to me. I told them about losing my contact. I told them about hiding in the girls' room. They thought it was hilarious.

"That's even worse than this party I went to with my cousin," said Tanya when she'd stopped laughing enough to be able to speak. "The minute we got there, he disappeared to play pool in the basement and left me sitting there all by myself for the next four hours with a bunch of strangers. The only person who was friendly to me was the dog."

Maria, giggling, shook her head. "That's nothing. When we first moved here my mother got one of the neighbours to invite me to her daughter's barbecue." She blushed just thinking about it. "I was so humiliated I couldn't even get up the courage to ask where the bathroom was." She bit into a fry. "The best thing that happened was that I fell into the pool and had to go home."

Marva wiped tears of laughter from her eyes. "Wait'll you hear about my sister's wedding," she gasped. "My mother made me wear a pink dress! You know, with ruffles and stuff?"

I didn't think I'd ever find anything about Saturday funny, but somehow talking to the Martians made it seem different. By the time the bell rang at the end of lunch, we were all in hysterics. I couldn't remember the last time I'd laughed so much.

* * *

"I don't know why you're getting mad at me," Amy complained. "It's not my fault you had a lousy time at the dance."

I took a potato chip from the bag I was holding. "I wasn't blaming you. I was just telling you, that's all."

Amy looked annoyed. "Oh, no you weren't, Jenny Kaliski," she said. "You were blaming me. I've known you long enough to know when you're whining."

Amber was home with a cold, and Kim had to go to the dentist, so Amy and I were walking home together on Monday afternoon. I'd felt so much better after talking to the Martians that instead of ducking when I saw Amy coming towards me, I stopped and waited. I'd felt so much better, in fact, that when Amy started to discuss the dance, I didn't look blank. Instead, apparently, I started to whine.

I couldn't help feeling that she was being a little unfair, accusing me of whining. She, after all, was the one who'd had a "cool", an "excellent" and a "fantastic" time. She was the one who couldn't remember when she'd had so much fun. She was the one who'd danced with three different boys. She was the one Dawyne Miller had asked to go to the movies. The one Rosie Henley had invited to her Hallowe'en party. The one who had to laugh when she thought about what she used to be like when she was a little kid way back in middle school. I was the one who'd spent the night sitting on a toilet bowl.

"I was not whining," I snapped back. "All I said was that I thought you could have stayed with me. I mean, we did go together, didn't we? I didn't want to go to the stupid dance in the first place. I only went because you asked me."

Amy's expression changed from annoyed to very annoyed. "For Pete's sake, Jen," she snapped, "it wasn't a *date*, you know. We just drove there together. All I was doing was trying to help you settle into high school. I never said I was going to hold your hand through the whole dance."

"You didn't say you were going to abandon me, either." I hadn't meant to say that, it just slipped out. But now that I had said it, I wasn't sorry. After all, it was the truth, wasn't it? If you couldn't tell your best friend the truth, who could you tell?

"Abandon you?" Amy's look went from very annoyed to stunned with disbelief mixed with outrage. She stopped dead. "What are you talking about, *abandon you*? I went to talk to some of my *other* friends, and when I turned around *you* were gone."

The whole thing had seemed pretty funny when I was telling the Martians about it, but it suddenly didn't seem that funny any more.

"You left me," I said. "You went off with your *other*

friends, and you left me alone." Maybe I hadn't been whining before, but even I could hear that I was whining now. "Why did you just walk off like that?" I moaned. "Why didn't you come back for me?"

Amy snorted. "And do what? Sit on the bleachers all night, watching everyone else have a good time?" She started marching ahead of me.

So she hadn't completely forgotten about me! She'd seen me sitting there all by myself on the bleachers like I had some contagious disease. She'd known all along I was waiting for her to come back. "You could've called me over," I reasoned. "I could've hung out with you and Kim and Amber."

Amy was so far ahead that she didn't hear me.

I raised my voice. "You didn't have to leave me all alone," I went on. "I don't know why when you're with Kim and Amber you can't be with me too. It's not like you all belong to some secret society."

She stopped and turned around. Our eyes met.

"Well, is it?"

"What do you want me to say, Jen?" asked Amy.

What did I want her to say? What was that supposed to mean? "I don't want you to say anything," I said. "I just want you to tell me why you never hang out with me when you're with *them*."

Amy made a face. "Really, Jen? You really want me to tell you?"

"Yes, Amy. I do." I nodded. After all, she was my best friend, I could tell her the truth and she could tell me the truth.

She frowned as if she didn't speak English that well and was trying to make sure she had understood what I'd said. "You're sure?"

Suddenly I had this truly bad feeling. It was the sort of feeling you get just as your mother's camera, which you weren't supposed to take out of the house in the first place, jumps out of your hands and into the pool. Like you knew all along this was going to happen. That if only you could go back a few minutes in time everything would be all right again. It was on the tip of my tongue to say no, I don't really want you to tell me. But I didn't. I said, "Well…"

Amy dropped her book bag on the ground. She folded her arms. "OK," she said in a flat voice. "I'll tell you, Jen. It's because they don't want to be seen with you."

I don't know why, but I smiled. Maybe I was hoping that she was kidding. You know, that she'd punch me on the arm and say, "Oh don't be silly, Jen, you know I'm only winding you up." Or maybe it was some sort of nervous reaction. I said, "Me?"

She nodded. "Yes, you. You're just not the kind of girl they like to hang around with."

"Why not?" I asked. "You can tell me. Is it my second head or is it my tail?"

She didn't smile. She shrugged. "It's everything."

I pretended to wipe the sweat from my forehead. "Oh, *everything*!" All of a sudden, my voice was shaking. "Well, that's a relief. I was worried it might be something major."

"Don't go twisting my words," said Amy. "You know that I don't mean *everything*."

"Well, what do you mean? Almost everything?"

"Look at yourself," she ordered, gesturing from my head to my feet. "Just look."

I looked at Amy, tall and thin and pretty, wearing a bright blue sweatshirt and flowered leggings. I looked down at myself, not tall, not thin and not pretty, wearing baggy jeans and a flannel shirt with a mustard stain and potato chip crumbs down the front.

I raised my chin. "So?"

"So you don't fit in. You don't act right. You don't look right. You—"

"No, you!" I shouted. I wanted to grab her curly blonde hair and yank it out of her head. "What about *you*? Am I the kind of girl *you* don't want to hang around with?"

Amy opened her mouth and closed it again.

"Well?" I screamed. "Am I?" When she still didn't say anything, I started walking away. Quickly.

"Don't start sulking!" Amy shouted after me.

"I'm not sulking!" I screamed back. Which was true. I'd passed sulking and was about to hit crying.

She came after me. "Jen," she said, "Jen, listen to me, I'm not telling you all this to hurt your feelings, you know. I'm your best friend. I'm trying to help you."

"Oh, thank you," I answered. "That makes me feel a lot better."

"I mean it, Jen, I am. What else are friends for? If I can't tell you the truth, who can?" She touched my shoulder. "Don't you see, Jen?" she continued. "High school is our big chance to start over. We can make new friends, we can do different things. You and I were nobodies in middle school, but now we can really belong."

I'd been right. Amy and her new pals were part of a secret society. The secret society of Miss Perfect Teenagers.

"You mean *you* can," I answered. "I'm the one who has everything wrong with her."

"But you don't have to," said Amy eagerly. "You could change. You could get some nice clothes. You could lose a few pounds. You could wear make-up. You could fix your hair. There's a lot you could do."

I was racing down the street, trying not to burst into tears, listening to my best friend list the hundreds of ways I could improve myself.

"I'm only telling you this for your own good, you know," Amy said when she'd finally finished. "You do know that, don't you, Jen?"

"Oh, sure," I mumbled. "I know." But inside I was wondering, Why did people have best friends? Why didn't they just have enemies? *It would be a whole lot less confusing.*

The rest of the way home Amy talked about cheerleading while I listened and tried to act like everything was the same as ever. We were both pretty relieved when we got to her road. She stood there for a few seconds, swinging her book bag. "Oh, yeah," she said, not quite looking at me, "Kim's mother is going to be giving me a lift to school from now on, so you don't have to wait for me in the morning."

I started walking. "Thanks for telling me," I said.

"And don't forget I have cheerleading practice after school the next two days," she called after me.

I didn't turn around. "Don't worry, I won't forget."

"See you!" she shouted.

I started down the street. *Oh, sure,* I thought, *see you in my dreams!*

I walked fast. I walked fast because I wanted to get home and into the safety of my room. So far I'd managed not to cry, but there was no guarantee that that would last.

But I also walked fast because suddenly I had this idea that everybody was watching me.

"You see that man over there?" I asked myself.

"Where?" I answered.

"Over *there*."

"Oh, over there. Yeah, I see him. He's washing his car."

I shook my head. "He's only pretending to wash his car," I informed myself. "Really, he's looking at you."

"At *me*?" I said. "Don't be ridiculous, he's not looking at *me*. He's getting the bird poop off his bumper."

"Of course he's watching you," I hissed back. "Just look at him! Look! He's nodding at you! He's thinking, *That girl should really do something about her hair. And look at those clothes...*"

I wasn't going to give in to panic. I started walking a little faster. "Oh, yeah," I replied. "And I suppose that woman playing ball with her kids is looking at me, too."

"That's right," I said. "Look! She just smiled at you! She's thinking *Good grief, that poor girl. I hope none of my children turn out like that.*"

I tried to sooth myself. "You're letting Amy get to you," I said. "That's all. You shouldn't pay any attention to her. You don't have to look like Rosie Henley to be a worthwhile person."

"Look!" I shrieked to myself. "Did you see that? That curtain just moved!"

I looked again. The curtain had moved. "It was probably just a cat or some—"

"Cat, my grandmother's dentures!" I practically shouted. "Don't you understand? Everybody's acting like they're inside their houses, reading their papers and watching football, but really they're peering through their curtains, watching you!"

"They're not," I protested. "It's statistically impossible that nobody in Red Bay has anything better to do than—"

"And you know what they're saying to each other? They're saying, 'Quick! Come over here! Isn't that Jenny Kaliski? Remember what a pretty baby she was? Remember what an adorable little girl? Well, look at her now! Her poor parents. It's a wonder they let her out in daylight.'"

By the time I got home I was a nervous wreck. I pretty much ran into the house and into my room. I locked the door. There was a series of thumps as Percy threw himself against it. I unlocked the door again and let him in. He jumped into my arms. At least he was glad to see me. "You love me, no matter what I look like, don't you Perce?" I asked him. He licked my face. Even though my mother doesn't believe in dogs on the furniture, Percy and I lay down on the bed together. I spent the rest of the afternoon going over and over what Amy had said. Percy fell asleep.

"Mom," I said to my mother later that night. "Mom, do you think I'm fat?"

I was washing and my mother was drying. She didn't look over at me as she lifted a handful of knives and forks from the drainer.

"Of course you're not fat," said my mother. "Where did you ever get an idea like that?"

But I knew my mother well enough to know how tricky she could be with language. She had me believing in Santa Claus for years because any time I'd ask her if there was a Santa she'd say, "Well, look around you, honey. What do you think?"

"OK," I said. "Not fat. But do you think I could stand to lose a few pounds?"

This time my mother looked over at me. "What for?" she wanted to know.

What for? What for did she think? "So I'd be thinner," I explained patiently.

"You don't need to be thinner," said my mother. "You're just the right weight for your height."

For some reason, this information didn't really cheer

me up. "But don't you think I'd look taller if I were thinner?" I probed.

My mother took a bowl from the dish drainer. "You might look taller if you walked on stilts, too," she said, smiling, "but I think you might have trouble getting into the back of the car."

"But, Mom——" I began.

"But, Jenny," my mother interrupted. "You're a very attractive young woman." She put her hand on my shoulder. She looked into my eyes. "Believe me," she said. "You're just fine the way you are."

"Dad," I said to my father later that night. "Dad, do you think I'm fat?" My mother was on the telephone in the kitchen, and we were in the living-room watching television. Well, my dad was watching television. Normally, I liked the same stuff he liked to watch, which was mainly science and nature programmes, but tonight the only thing I could think about was my body.

My father said, "Uh."

"Dad," I repeated. "Dad, do you think I'm fat?"

My father was watching something about birds of the Amazon. He's as nuts about birds as I am about planets. He doesn't even care if the birds aren't doing anything very interesting – you know, if they're just eating bugs or something. He told me this show was fascinating. He was wrong. The bird the narrator was talking about now was called a hoatzin. It didn't even eat bugs, it ate leaves. How's that for interesting? It was the weirdest bird I'd ever seen. My father's eyes didn't leave the screen. He thought the hoatzin was beautiful. "Fat?" he asked. "Who's fat?"

"Dad!" I shouted. "Dad, listen to me. Do you think I'm fat?"

He turned in my direction. "What?"

"Fat," I repeated for what seemed like the zillionth time. "Do you think I'm fat?"

"You?" He looked at me as though he'd never seen me before.

Good grief, I thought, *it's a miracle he and my mother ever got married. Every time he turned his back on her he probably forgot what she looked like.*

"Yes," I said, "me. Do you think I need to lose a few pounds?"

"Are you kidding?" My father grinned. "You don't need to lose any weight, Jen. You look great."

"But I'm short," I reminded him.

"Short but perfectly formed," said my father.

"But, Dad, if I lost—"

"Just a minute, Jen," said my father, distracted by something flapping on the screen. "This is a crucial moment."

While my mother talked to her sister on the phone about her sister's latest home improvements, and my father watched semi-flightless birds on TV, I went into my parents' room. I stood in front of the full-length mirror. It wasn't like I'd never looked at myself before. I'd looked at myself a trillion times. But not like this.

I twisted to the left. I twisted to the right. My thighs really did wobble. And my bottom looked like a watermelon. How could a person who wore "petite" have such a big bottom?

I stepped forward. I stepped back. I'd known I was no great beauty or anything, but it hadn't ever bothered me before. Not really. Only that time Miss Marilu hadn't let me be the fairy princess. That had hurt. But that had been when I was nine. I'd figured I was pretty normal now. But maybe I wasn't. Maybe I'd gotten used to being me. A misfit. A geek.

I turned to the left. I turned to the right. I stepped forward. I stepped backward. I shook my legs. I waved my arms. Maybe Amy was right. Maybe if I lost a few pounds, and did something with my hair, and had myself stretched, I could look perfect too. I turned around again. Or maybe not.

Inside Martian Control

Don't get me wrong. I knew I was never going to be a Miss Perfect Teenager. My hair wasn't going to suddenly turn curly and blonde. My teeth weren't going to suddenly look like a movie star's. I would never wear a size six. No matter how much I prayed it was unlikely that I was going to grow. And it's not like I even wanted to be Miss Perfect Teenager. I mean, *me*? I mean, who wants to spend their Saturdays jumping around a football field in shorts screaming, "Red Bay! Red Bay! Show them the way!"? If I wanted to be anything while I was in high school, I wanted to be a lifeguard. And afterwards, of course, I wanted to be an astrophysicist. Those were the things that were important to me, not being pretty and popular. I told myself that several times in the next couple of days, so I knew it was true.

* * *

But after my talk with Amy – or Amy's talk with me, to be more exact – I began to have this fantasy of waking up one morning and discovering that I was incredibly beautiful and thin. I was even sort of blonde. I could just picture the look on people's faces as I strolled into school.

"Who is *that*?" they'd all be whispering to one another. Kim and Amber would be tripping over themselves trying to meet me. Rosie Henley would invite me to her Hallowe'en party, but I wouldn't be sure if I could go. The most popular kids in the school would be fighting to have me sit at their lunch table. "Please," they'd beg me, "don't sit with those Martians, sit with us." I'd be asked out on a date. Maybe not even just one date. Maybe I'd be asked on three or four. Amy would dump Kim and Amber to hang out with me again. It'd be like Cinderella transformed by her fairy godmother, but without the coach and horses and those dumb glass shoes.

So I decided that though I wasn't going to become one of those girls who thinks about nothing but boys and clothes, I would improve myself a little. There was no harm in that. There were things I could do without too much trauma.

The first thing was I could go on a diet. After all, thin was the one thing that *everyone* wanted to be. Not everybody looked good with curly hair. Not everybody looked good in cycling shorts. But everybody looked good thin. And I was sure that what I'd told my mother was right. If I were thinner, I'd look taller. Tall and thin. My fantasy shimmered before my eyes. There I was, striding up the path to school. Boys were nudging each other. Girls were hugging. "Good grief!" they were whispering. "I know who that is!" It's Jenny Kaliski! Who would've guessed how attractive she really is?"

I know this must sound weird, but even though I was fourteen, I'd never been on a diet before. My mother and Amy's mother and all their friends and relatives had been on diets. A lot of the girls from school had been on diets. And I knew from magazines and movies and television that everybody diets most of the time. But I'd never been on a diet. I decided to keep it a secret. I was going to surprise everyone. Especially Amy. I couldn't wait to see her face. I figured I'd spend a week or so being careful about what I ate – you know, no chips, no butter, no soda, no sweets – and then one morning I'd wake up, just like in my fantasy, and none of my clothes would fit me any more. It was going to be really easy.

"You want some cakes?" asked Sue, pushing a paper plate full of squares of something iced and chocolate towards me.

We were just finishing lunch. Or those of us who weren't on a secret diet were finishing lunch. Those of us who were on a secret diet were nibbling slowly on a carrot stick, chewing every bite twenty-six times. "No, thanks," I said.

"My mother made it," said Sue.

"Sue's mother makes great chocolate cake," said Tanya.

"I'm sure it's terrific," I said, "but I'm really full…"

Joan raised one eyebrow. "Full? From what? You've hardly eaten anything."

"Well, if Jenny doesn't want her piece, I'll take it," said Tanya. "I'm starving."

She reached for the cake, but Sue slapped her hand. "Starving?" shrieked Sue. "Tanya, you never stop eating long enough to know what it feels like to be slightly hungry." She pushed the cake towards me again. "Come on, Jenny, my mother always gives me enough for everybody."

"Don't tell me we've got another Marva on our hands," said Maria, laughing. Marva had already refused some cake because she didn't want to poison her body with sugar.

Marva smirked. "Laugh all you want," she said to Maria. "But I'll be the one who laughs last."

"Just take a little," urged Sue.

I looked at the square of cake in front of me. It was really dark chocolate and the icing was white, just the way I liked it best. I could practically taste it in my mouth, all soft and crumbling with sweet and grainy icing. On Monday I'd had one bowl of cereal for breakfast. I'd had one sandwich and an apple for lunch. I'd had one helping of supper, no salad dressing, no potato, no butter and no dessert. No snacks. Today was Tuesday. I'd had two pieces of dry toast for breakfast, and a sandwich and a carrot for lunch. On the one hand, I didn't want to go off my diet already, not when I was doing so well. On the other hand, maybe Tanya really wasn't starving, but I was.

"Oh, go ahead," Joan said. "It's not going to kill you, is it?"

"That's what you think," said Marva.

I looked at the cake. It wasn't a very big piece. How many calories could there be in one tiny, infinitesimal piece of chocolate cake? Hadn't I passed up ice-cream last night? Ice-cream *and* mashed potatoes? "Well…"

"Oh, go ahead," said Sue. "If you don't like it, Tanya will finish it for you."

I was weakening. I could feel it. That piece of cake was calling to me. "Jenny," it was saying, "Jenny, I'm small. You can eat me and it won't make any difference. What's dry toast compared to double fudge?" When you're weakening you need something to hold on to. I looked around the table. Maybe I could use a little support on my diet after all. Maybe keeping it a secret wasn't the best thing I could do. Amy's mother always told everyone when she went on a diet, even people she didn't know very well. I'd thought she did that so they'd be sure to tell her she looked thinner. Now I realized it was so they'd stop her from eating.

I leaned forward. "The thing is," I said, keeping my voice down and trying to sound casual, "well … you see the thing is, I'm sort of on a diet." I might as well have waved a banner and shot off fireworks. They all began to shout at once.

"A diet?" howled Sue. "To lose weight, you mean?"

"You're nuts," boomed Marva, "diets just make you fat."

"Oh, Jenny," said Maria, "you don't need to lose weight. You're just right."

"You?" Tanya practically fell off her chair. "What are you on a diet for? If anybody should be on a diet it's me."

"Did you know there are celebrities who've been on diets for twenty years?" asked Sue.

"What kind of diet?" asked Joan.

I looked at her. "What?"

"What kind of diet?" Joan repeated. "Calorie, fibre, fat or carbohydrate? Are you eating one type of food, substituting nutritional shakes for meals or following menu plans?"

I didn't know what she was talking about. "Well … I … well … I'm not really being that strict about it."

"Oh, but you have to be," said Joan, "or you won't get anywhere. My sister's been on every diet there's ever been. Diets where you eat all the calories you want, but nothing before noon. Diets where you only eat a thousand calories, not one more or one less. The ice-cream diet, the kumquat and spring-water diet, the spinach diet, the wholewheat-bread diet…"

To tell you the truth, I was amazed. This may sound naïve, but I really wasn't aware of just how many different diets there were to go on. I guess I thought everybody followed Amy's mother's diet: the Hide All the Good Stuff and Scrape the Cheese From Your Pizza diet. It wasn't so much a diet as a system of denial. You ate less of everything you wanted and none of the things you liked best.

"And do they work?" I asked.

Marva gave me a pitying look. "Oh, sure they do," she said, smirking again. "That's why Joan's sister goes on so many of them."

Joan gave Marva a non-pitying look. She turned back to me with a shrug. "Some of them do," she said. "And some of them don't. I wouldn't know, personally." Joan was built like a stick insect. "But I do know that you have to be on one or the other. You can't leave this sort of thing to chance."

I watched Tanya scoop up my piece of cake and shovel it in her mouth. I don't even think she chewed it. "I can't?" I said.

Joan was adamant. "No, you can't." She licked some icing from her fingers. "Dieting is a serious business."

"I wouldn't mind the chocolate cake diet," said Sue.

"You are what you eat," said Marva.

Tanya began to laugh. "I'm pepperoni pizza and Rocky Road ice-cream!" she roared. "I'm chocolate-chip brownies and double-cheese-burgers!"

Marva threw a bean sprout at her. "You're a monument to junk food, that's what you are."

Maria leaned across the table towards me. "You don't need to diet, Jenny. Really. My mother says boys like girls to have a little meat on their bones."

Well, that certainly made me feel better. "Maybe I should pick up a calorie counter or something like that on my way home today," I mused.

Marva put one long white hand on my shoulder. Her purple nails and silver bangles sparkled. "Not today," said Marva. "Today you're coming home with me, remember?"

I stared into those large dark eyes for a second. I

hadn't remembered; I'd forgotten. Well, maybe not forgotten exactly. Blanked out of my mind entirely might be closer to the truth. Last night Marva had called me up and invited me over to her house after school. "I've been thinking about frogs," she said, "and I may have a couple of ideas." For some reason – probably because I was weak with hunger at the time – I'd said yes. Even though going into Martian Control was just about the last thing in the world that I wanted to do. I mean, if they had bats on the outside of the house, what did they have on the inside?

I glanced around the table. Everyone was looking at me. I couldn't very well get out of it now.

"Oh … uh … sure," I stammered. "Of course. I remember." I smiled at the three silver hoops in Marva's left ear. "I'm really looking forward to it."

On the way to her house, Marva did most of the talking. Marva was never shy, but today she wouldn't shut up. She told me how much she wanted to be an actress, though she wasn't sure that she'd ever want to do television – it was the theatre that really mattered. She told me that her mother had wanted to be a dancer when she was a teenager, but she'd injured her back. She told me that her father had lived in India for three years after he got out of college. She told me that her older sister had disappointed her parents by marrying a banker. She told me that her brother used to have a pet iguana. She asked me if I believed in astral projection.

"Astral projection?" I knew a lot about stars, I mean, stars are my thing, but I wasn't sure what astral projection was.

Marva said it was when you left your body. You were still you, but you could fly around and see yourself.

I said, "You're kidding, right?"

"Uh uh," said Marva. "It's one of my great ambitions in life. Next to acting on the London stage."

She asked me what my great ambition was. For some reason – maybe because I was so surprised she was giving me a chance to talk – I told her something I'd never told anybody but Amy before. "What I'd really like to do is go into space," I said. "You know, I'd like to be a scientist-astronaut."

Marva nodded. "It's sort of the same thing," she said.

I wasn't so sure about that, but I didn't have a chance to reply because we'd arrived at her house.

Most places look better in the sunshine than they do in heavy rain. You know: brighter, cheerier, less likely to be inhabited by vampires or visitors from outer space. But not the house where Marva lived. It looked just as weird on a sunny afternoon as it had in the rain. Weirder even. In the sunlight you could see just how badly the paint was peeling, and just how much junk was on the porch, and that there were all sorts of feeders and bat boxes and bird houses and wind chimes and *things* hanging from the roof and the trees.

"Home sweet home," cried Marva as she stepped over a sleeping cat and sailed through the front door.

So this is it, I thought to myself. *Buckle your seat belt! You're going inside Martian Control!*

"Yeah." I smiled, stepping over the same cat and following her in. "Home sweet home." Two inches over the threshold, I tripped over something large and warm and soft. I flew past Marva. Whatever I'd tripped over let out this bloodcurdling scream and flew past me. I pulled myself off the wall.

Marva didn't even notice. "Come on," she said, continuing down the hall. "My room's a mess. We can go into the dining-room."

Still shaking slightly, I groped down the dark hall after her.

My grandmother had a dining-room. My grandmother's dining room has a big cupboard, and a sideboard, and an enormous table in the middle of the room. The one thing you do in my grandmother's dining-room is eat. One glance at Marva's dining room told me that the one thing you *didn't* do in it was eat. True, the table was large and in the middle of the room, but it was piled high with who-knew-what. Bags, boxes, pieces of wood, books, tools, empty cups and glasses… There were only two chairs, and both of them were covered with papers and clothes. Marva's room must really have been a mess if we had to come in here.

Marva threw her books on top of something on the table. "You want some juice or food?" she asked as she pulled out a chair and shoved the things on it onto the floor.

My stomach growled. "Oh, no thanks," I said. "I'm fine."

"Take a seat, then," said Marva, indicating the other chair. "I need sustenance. I'm going to get myself something to eat. I'll be right back."

I removed a stack of wood and a hammer from the second chair and sat down. Gingerly. I looked around the room. The walls were lined with bookcases – though they weren't all filled with books. Most of them were filled with junk. There was an open sewing machine in one corner and some sort of workbench in another. There was an enormous fish tank, another tank of small reptiles and a cage of mice under the window. There were posters of things like whales and tree toads hanging on the shelves and the few bare pieces of wall. There was a wood carving of a snowy owl on top of one of the bookcases. I'd never seen anything like this room before.

Marva came thumping back in with a tray in her hands. On it was a bottle of juice, two glasses, a bowl of fruit and a bowl of nuts. She threw herself into her chair. She kicked off her shoes. She scooped up a handful of nuts and started crunching away. Suddenly I felt like I hadn't eaten in weeks. I had to bite my tongue to stop myself from reaching for an orange or two.

"OK," said Marva, shovelling another handful of nuts into her mouth, "let's talk about frogs."

Frog's legs, I thought. *I wonder if they really do taste like chicken?*

Marva started to talk. Though not about frogs. She said she hoped I hadn't traumatized the dog too much by stepping on him or she'd never get him out of the bath tub. She talked about amino acids. She told me about a woman in Arizona who could leave her body at will.

While Marva talked, I listened. Not that there was anything else to do. At first I thought that I was going to sit there, counting every nut she put in her mouth because I was so hungry, but my hunger was soon replaced by something else. Paranoia. The more Marva talked, the more uneasy I became. I was sure I was being watched. I could feel two eyes boring into me. Just like when I was walking home from Amy's on Sunday. I looked around, but the fish were minding their own business, swimming in circles, the lizards were sound asleep, and the mice were out of range.

Marva talked some more about the theatre, and how the part she'd really like to play was Hamlet.

"Hamlet?" I said, trying to distract myself. "But Hamlet's a man."

"So what?" said Marva. "It's called *acting,* isn't it?"

Then she told me the names of the two lizards and the fifteen fish and how her brother had once walked halfway to Connecticut because someone told him that he would never be able to do it. "He would've made it, too," said Marva, "except my father figured out where he was going and went after him in the car."

Then she told me about the time she and Joan had snuck out of the house at midnight to go for a walk in the moonlight, but when they'd comeback they couldn't get in and had to climb up a tree and in through her brother's bedroom window.

"You and *Joan*?" I said. Joan was nice, but she seemed so boring. I could imagine Marva doing something wild like sneaking out of the house to walk under the stars, but not Joan. It made me feel almost jealous. The most daring thing Amy and I had ever done together was go on the Death Defier roller-coaster at Playworld after our mothers had told us not to.

"It was a full moon," said Marva.

Although Marva was actually pretty interesting, I was getting more and more nervous. Not only was the house strange, but I was becoming surer and surer that I was being watched. Trying not to be too obvious, I kept glancing around, but I couldn't see anyone. The lizards were still fast asleep.

An apple core went whizzing past my ear. "Pay attention," ordered Marva. "You're not paying attention."

"Yes, I am."

Marva tossed her head. "I've decided what you should do about the frogs," she said grandly.

Relief washed over me. It was about time. Once she'd told me her idea, I'd be able to go home. I stopped listening for shallow breathing and looking for eyes peering at me from the shadows. "Great," I said. "What should I do?"

Marva grinned. "You should set all of the frogs in Mr Hererra's lab free," she announced.

"I should what?" She really was too much.

"Set them all free," Marva repeated. "It'll be like the Boston Tea Party, a symbolic revolutionary act."

"I don't want to start a revolution," I pointed out. "I just don't want to have to cut up a frog."

Marva waved her arms theatrically. "But just think of it!" she cried. "If you give them their freedom, no one will have to cut one up. You'll not only be stopping the senseless slaughter of innocent amphibians, you'll be contributing to the happiness of your fellow students." She leaned back in her chair with a contented sigh. "Actually, it's exactly what my brother once did."

My mind had started wandering again while she was talking about innocent amphibians, but the mention of her brother brought it back with a snap. Marva's brother! Chris "Bizarro" County! Of course! Why hadn't I thought of that before? That was why I thought someone was watching us! Somebody *was* watching us. Marva's weirdo brother. He was probably hidden behind a bookcase or peeking through a crack in the door or something.

"Oh, really?" I said, smiling at Marva and acting as though I was about to lean back in my chair. But then, quick as an electron, I spun around, sure that I'd catch him off guard.

I was in mid-spin when I heard it. Flapping. The flapping of heavy wings. *Bats!* I thought. The flapping grew louder. *Good grief! They've got bats in the house!* Now I had my back to Marva and was staring at a wall of books. All I could think of was bats. Big bats with tiny red eyes and enormous leather wings.

Swooshswooshswooo ... Swooshswooshswooo...
The flapping was right over me.

"Get down!" shouted Marva.

I didn't get down. Something skimmed past my head. Something large. Something with claws and fangs.

I screamed. It screamed. I screamed again. It was flapping above me, trying to land in my hair. I jumped out of my chair and started running from the room. As I crashed through the door, I could hear Marva start to sob. I ran down the hallway, shrieking. I had to get to the front door. That was all. I just had to get to the door. Once I was outside I'd be safe. Whatever it was was right behind me, shrieking louder than I. I ran and ran. Flapflapflapflapflap. Swooshswooshswoosh... It was the longest hallway I'd ever been in. It was the hallway of a nightmare, getting longer and longer as you run faster and faster. Flapflapflapflapswooshswooshswooo...

Then, just as I was about to reach the County's front door, it flew open, and a tall figure stepped inside. *A vampire!* I thought. *A vampire has come to help the bat!*

"Geronimo!" screamed the vampire. "Geronimo!"

And then I slammed into him at full speed and the two of us fell to the floor.

Marva's laughter filled up the hall.

"Get off me, you idiot!" screamed the figure in the

doorway. But it wasn't a vampire trying to stop me from escaping, it was Marva's brother trying to get into the house. It was easy to see why he was always in trouble in school. He had a real attitude problem.

"Oh, pardon me," I said with as much sarcasm as I could manage under the circumstances. "The next time I'm being attacked, I'll try and make sure that you're not in my way." It seemed to me that he could have asked if I was all right or not. He was at least a foot taller than I was. I touched my nose to see if it was bleeding.

"What are you, deaf as well as stupid? Get up! I have to get Geronimo! Can't you understand you've upset him?"

I'd been planning to get up. I mean, I wasn't going to just lie there in the hallway, sprawled across Chris County, was I? I'd rather have been back at the dance. But his attitude was really beginning to annoy me. What did he mean *I'd* upset Geronimo? His bat had frightened me out of a year's growth, which was something a person of my height couldn't afford.

I didn't budge. If he could have an attitude, I could have one too. "*I've* upset *him*? And what about me? I'm not used to having vampire bats chasing me through the house."

"Deaf, stupid and blind as well," he said. "Geronimo isn't a bat, he's a snowy owl." He gave me a shove.

"Don't you shove me!" I shoved him back.

He looked like he was going to just lift me off him, but Marva finally recovered enough to speak. "Stop it, you guys," she ordered. "You don't even know each other yet and already you're fighting." She bent over us. "Jenny," she said in this mock-formal way, "I'd like you to meet my brother, Chris. Chris, this is Jenny Kaliski. Remember I told you about her? She's the one having trouble with Herrera."

The annoyed expression that had been on his face since we landed on the floor was replaced by one of amazement. "*This* is frog girl?"

Frog girl? Was that what Marva called me at home? For Pete's sake, I might be short but I wasn't green.

He turned to me. The annoyed look returned. "How could you scare Geronimo like that?" he demanded. "I thought you were concerned about other species."

I pulled myself to a sitting position and glared at him. I could think of one species I wasn't feeling too concerned about. "I'll have you know that your precious owl nearly scared me to death."

He got to his feet and stood there glaring at me. "Maybe next time he'll do better" he said. What a charming boy.

"You could help her up, you know," said Marva.

"I don't need your help," I informed him coolly.

But of course, Chris County wasn't the kind of person to care what anyone else said. He reached out, grabbed my arm and pulled me to my feet so quickly that we both nearly fell down again. "As soon as I find Geronimo you can apologize," he said.

Me apologize to an *owl*? I was too surprised to answer. Marva and I watched him disappear up the stairs, making what I supposed must be comforting snowy owl sounds and calling, "Geronimo! Geronimo! It's all right, boy, that girl won't scare you any more."

Marva turned to me with a big grin. "Isn't it great Chris came home?" she asked. "Now he'll be able to help with your frog plans."

"Marva," I said. "Marva, is that what you call me? 'Frog girl'?"

Marva laughed. "Of course not," she said. "That's what Chris calls you."

War

By the time I got to lunch the next day, the Martians had all heard the story of my run-in with the Abominable Bat about sixteen times. They thought it was hilarious. Especially the part where the hand-raised owl and I went tearing down the hallway and I knocked Chris County flat on his back.

"You should've seen her face!" Marva howled. "I wish I'd had a camera."

Tanya was running back and forth behind my chair, holding her sweater stretched out like wings. "Waooohwaoooh," she mimicked, "it's the giant bat come to get you…"

"Very funny," I said. I was the only one who wasn't laughing. Even Maria, who could usually be counted on for sympathy and understanding, was wiping tears from her eyes. "You should be on the stage, Tanya," I said sweetly. And then I added, "The one that left an hour ago."

Tanya's mature response to this was to stick out her tongue at me and squawk. "It's sort of like Goliath being felled by David, isn't it?" roared Tanya.

"It was more like Arnold Schwarzenegger tripping over Danny DeVito," Marva roared back.

Maria put her arm around me. "Oh, come on, Jen," she coaxed. "Even you have to admit that it must've been pretty funny." So much for sympathy and understanding.

"No, I don't," I replied. "I don't have to admit any such thing." I opened my corn chips. Not only was I embarrassed, but I was off my diet as well. I'd promised myself that after school I was going into town to pick up a diet book and start over, but at the moment I was still recovering from the shock and trauma of spending an afternoon in Martian Control. I hadn't been able to stop eating since I'd gotten home last night. I'd walked through my back door, gone straight to the kitchen cabinet, taken down a box of cookies and inhaled the whole thing just standing there, leaning against the counter. I could see my mother eyeing me as I wolfed down cookie after cookie, wondering whether or not this was a sign of drug addiction.

"I can't believe you didn't warn her about Geronimo," Joan said to Marva. "I mean, you can't blame her for getting a little upset when this owl swooped down on her…" She'd been struggling to look serious, but at the mention of swooping owls she dissolved into giggles again.

Marva widened her eyes innocently. "She must have seen him sitting up there," she protested. "What did she think he was? A parakeet?"

Tanya flapped behind me some more. "Tweettweettweettweettweet."

"I told you," I repeated for about the hundredth time, "I thought he was a carving."

"What kind of owl is it again?" asked Sue.

Good grief. Trust Sue to be irrelevant. I gave her a look. "Big," I said. "Very, very big."

"And anyway," Marva went on, "the whole thing was Jenny's fault, jumping around in her seat like that. She frightened him."

Maria gave me a nudge. "Not as much as he frightened Jenny," she grinned.

Marva ignored this valid point. She waved a cucumber spear at me. "You're lucky my brother was so understanding," she continued. "He really loves that owl."

I rolled my eyes in mock amazement. "No kidding?" I said. "How can you tell?" You'd think I'd served it for Thanksgiving dinner or something, the way he'd carried on.

Tanya plopped back into her chair. "So I guess this

means Marva's brother isn't going to help you with Herrera, huh?" she winked.

Now there was a lucky guess. I shook my head. "Not in this millennium."

"Oh, don't exaggerate," said Marva. "He still might come around. Once he was sure Geronimo wasn't permanently traumatized, he thought the whole thing was pretty funny." She wiped some cucumber juice from her chin. "At least he told you not to waste time trying to figure out how to free the frogs," she said. "He didn't have to, you know. That was a favour."

Was it my imagination, or was she making it sound like freeing the frogs had been *my* idea?

"Why not?" asked Sue.

I looked at her again. It was like everyone else was having one conversation, and Sue was having another. "Because they're dead when they get here," I informed her. "They used to come still hopping and croaking, but since the time Chris let them loose in the biology pond behind the science building Mr Herrera makes sure they're all dead on arrival."

"What a shame," sighed Sue. "Those poor little frogs."

"What's the difference?" asked Tanya. "They're going to die anyway."

"Aren't we all?" asked Marva.

"Ugh," groaned Maria. "Do you think we could talk about something else while we're eating?"

"Like what?" Marva grinned in my direction. "Vampire bats?"

You might think so, but diets are a lot like stars.

If you didn't know anything about stars, you might look up at the sky over your house at night and see the Plough and a couple of other constellations you can't identify, and figure that's it. "That's it," you'd say to yourself. "There are a few hundred stars in the sky." Maybe a thousand if it's a clear night. If you live in a large city you'd probably think there are about two. Two stars, and one of them is a planet. You'd have no idea that the stars stretch on and on forever; billions and billions and billions of stars, in uncounted galaxies and innumerable solar systems, on and on and on.

Well, that's the way it is with diets. I'd thought there were maybe a couple of them. You know, maybe a dozen or so. I'd figured I'd go to Jones's Drugstore in Red Bay, where they have a special section just for books and magazines, and I'd buy myself a diet. Then I'd know where I was going, how I was getting there and roughly how long it was going to take. *Two Weeks to a Thinner You* – that sort of thing. Armed with something in writing, I wouldn't be as likely to stuff an entire box of cookies in my face every time some owl with a beak like a snow plough and a twenty-foot wingspan tried to land on my head.

It wasn't until I was actually standing in Jones's Drugstore, staring at the shelf labelled "Health and Beauty", that I realized what a mistake I'd made. It was like suddenly finding yourself in deepest space. The diet books stretched on and on for ever; dozens and dozens of diet books, big ones and small ones and ones you could stick in your pocket, on and on and on. What was worse, even though they all had different titles and stuff, they looked sort of the same. Like stars, I guess. They all had some smiling blonde in a leotard jumping for joy on the cover because she didn't have hips. And they were all recommended by some doctor. And they all had quotes from satisfied dieters on the back. And they all guaranteed a happier and healthier you.

"Good grief," I muttered out loud, "how are you supposed to know where to start?"

Overwhelmed, I edged over to the magazines. Maybe I could find something there. I was in luck. Every woman's magazine on the stand had a diet in it, too. "Lose Weight Before the Holidays," and "Stuff the Turkey, Not You," they ordered. "Ten Pounds in Ten Days," and "Get It Off and Keep It Off," they promised.

I edged back to the books. Fats? Carbohydrates? Calories? I tried to remember what Joan said about diets. All I could remember was that she said you have to have one. I tried to remember something my mother had said about diets. All I could remember were her famous last words, "Tomorrow. I'll start tomorrow."

In the end I took something called The Ultimate Dieter. I figured I couldn't go wrong with something "ultimate" in the title. It had a quote on the front from a doctor who said it was the one diet book you ever needed; and a quote on the back from a woman who said it had changed her life. *That's exactly what I need*, I thought. *To change my life.* And, just to be on the safe side, I bought two magazines as well.

On the way to the cash register to pay, I passed the Hair Care section. I picked up something called Natural Blonde. *Why not?* I asked myself. *If you're going to improve yourself, you might as well really do it.* The box said that by using this product you could gradually transform yourself from mousy to blonde in a few weeks. The box said it was easy, safe and impossible to tell from the real thing. *Perfect*, I thought. *I'll be the ultimate dieter and a natural blonde.*

The woman at the cash register raised an eyebrow when I handed her the book. "Don't tell me this is for *you*," she said with a smile. "Oh no," I said, smiling back. "It's for my mother."

Red Bay isn't exactly a metropolis. It isn't even a small town. It's a village. Being a village means that it doesn't even have a movie house any more. You have to go to the mall if you want to see a movie. But it does have a main street. And it does have a bay. And it was a really nice October afternoon. If this had been an afternoon last year, Amy and I would have been out on our bikes. But it wasn't last year, of course, it was this year, and Amy was practising scissor-kicks and splits. I decided to walk down to the bay and sit in the park for a while.

Except for a few squirrels and a couple of mothers pushing their little kids on the swings, the park was deserted. I sat on a bench near the dock and started flipping through the magazines I'd bought. I didn't really read many magazines, and when I did I usually read science and natural history magazines. You know, with pictures of solar eclipses and mosquitoes and scientists sitting around smiling like regular people, and long articles about what life was going to be like in the future, or used to be like a million years ago, or was like if you were a sea urchin. These magazine were nothing like that. Besides the hundreds of pictures of beautiful skinny women, laughing, they were filled with articles about how to take care of yourself, and improve yourself, and all the things that could go wrong. I'd never realized there was so much to worry about. Soap. Sun. Water. Air. Dry hair. Oily skin. Wearing the wrong colours. Wearing the wrong make-up. Flabby arms. Cellulite. Cellulite! I'd never even *thought* about cellulite before. "Cellulite and you," said my magazine. "No matter how young or thin you are, you're still not safe." And I'd thought I was!

I was sitting there, reading about the awful things that were going to happen to my thighs if I wasn't careful, when I heard a hoarse croaking sound. I can remember thinking, *That's funny, I never heard any frogs down here before*, but then an article on split ends caught my eye and I forgot about it. The croaking got louder. I didn't pay any attention. Split ends weren't the end of it. Stress could make you go bald. Bald! My father was going bald. I read on, to see if baldness was hereditary or not. The croaking got louder. *Boy*, I thought, *this is one big frog*. It got louder. It sounded like it was coming from my right. I slid over a little to the left. It got louder. This frog was practically screaming. I slid over some more. I think maybe I said something then. Something like, "Good grief, what kind of frog *is* this?" And that's when the frog really started going berserk. I dropped my magazine and jumped off the bench. I'd had enough run-ins with emotional wildlife already this week, I wasn't about to be attacked by some giant, shouting amphibian.

As soon as I was on my feet, cautiously looking around, the croaking turned to laughter. I froze. The laughter sort of exploded. I walked back to the bench and leaned over. There, squatting behind a tree, was Marva's brother. He waved. "Rititnitit, frog girl," he said, grinning.

I couldn't believe my eyes! I'd barely known the guy for twenty-four hours, and already he'd made a fool of me twice. "You!" I yelled. "What is it with you? Are you trying to give me a heart attack or what?"

He got to his feet, dusting off his jeans. "Did anybody ever tell you you have a very nervous disposition?"

Something inside of me snapped. It wasn't grown-up. It wasn't the way you acted in high school. It was probably the sort of behaviour that caused acne and cellulite. Not to mention baldness. If Kim, Amber or Rosie Henley had seen me, they would have known I was a lost cause. But I couldn't help myself. I had this overwhelming desire to inflict physical violence on Marva's brother. Without another thought I hurled myself at Chris County. It might have been the second time in two days that he'd humiliated me – but it was also the second time that I'd knocked him to the ground.

* * *

As it turned out, Chris wasn't that bad, really. He'd seen me sitting on the bench, and had actually come over to apologize for Geronimo's frightening me. He said that after he'd thought it over, he realized he'd been insensitive to my feelings. "Geronimo can be a little intimidating if you're not used to him," he admitted. "Even if you did overreact."

I don't know exactly how it happened, but one minute I wanted to hurt him, and the next minute we were lying side by side on the grass, yelling, "Rititnitit rititnitit" and laughing ourselves silly. So we decided to call a truce and go to Roth's Luncheonette for a soda. "Geronimo's treat," said Chris. "I think he owes you that much."

"There's only one way to fight Herrera," he said, sliding onto a stool, "and that's total open warfare."

I slid onto the stool next to him. "You mean you think I should shoot him?"

From the other side of the counter, I could see the waitress staring in our direction, thinking about us. For maybe the first time in my life, it didn't bother me that I was being watched. It didn't bother me because I knew she wasn't staring at me. She was staring at Chris. Not only was he very tall and thin with the same bony, sort of striking face and dark eyes as Marva, but he was the only boy in Red Bay who dressed all in black and wore a pony-tail *and* an earring, a silver bat.

Chris laughed. Marva's laugh was almost a cackle, Chris's was rolling and deep. "I wouldn't do anything that drastic," he said. "If you only wounded him he'd probably have you thrown in jail. He tried to get me kicked out of school just for putting a couple of frogs into the pond."

"Forty," I corrected.

He looked up at the menu on the wall. "Ok, forty," he admitted. "But they were small."

I studied the menu in silence for a few seconds, thinking.

"What's the matter?" he asked. "You changing your mind?"

I shrugged. "Not exactly," I said. "I mean, I still don't see any reason why I should have to cut up this frog. It's pointless – I haven't changed my mind about that. It's just that I don't know if I can really afford to get on Mr Herrera's bad side. He is head of the department, you know. And I want to major in physics in college. What if I don't do well in my science courses in high school?"

"Physics?" said Chris. "You want to major in physics?"

I nodded, slowly. "I'm going to be an astrophysicist."

Except for my father, no one took me very seriously about this. My grandfather was sure I'd grow out of it in time and decide to be a teacher or something. Even my mother thought it was a phase, like wanting to be a fishergirl when I was five. "It's the most exciting thing there is," I admitted. "Just thinking about it makes me happy."

Chris was shaking his head and laughing. I couldn't believe I'd thought he had a bad attitude.

"This is wild," said Chris. "I was interested in physics for a long time myself. I'm really into Einstein and Oppenheimer and Schrödinger and guys like that. But then I went back to my first love."

"Owls?" I ventured.

"Owls, bats, dogs, hippos, sloths, killer whales, frogs…"

"What'll it be?" asked the waitress.

I almost answered, "Zoologist." I hadn't seen her come over.

"I'll have a double-fudge sundae," said Chris.

"Hey, wait a minute," I protested. "I thought Marva didn't eat stuff like that."

He pointed to his reflection in the mirror on the opposite wall. "Do I look like Marva?" he asked.

"Yes," I said, "you do."

He snapped his fingers. "Ah, but *am* I Marva?"

We smiled at each other in the glass. *Well what do you know*, I was thinking, *maybe he isn't as weird as I thought.*

The waitress tapped her pencil. "Do I look like I have all day?" she asked.

What the heck, I decided. Tomorrow I'd start my diet. Today I could splurge. "I'll have a chocolate milkshake," I said.

Chris said that open warfare didn't have to involve bloodshed. He said that I should make my formal protest – a peaceful, public demonstration of my beliefs – and that if, in the end, I had to bow to Mr Herrera's power, at least I could do so with dignity.

"Just because I've made an enemy of Mr Herrera doesn't mean that you will," he reassured me.

I wasn't all that reassured. Mr Herrera wasn't particularly nice to people he *liked*. "An enemy?" I repeated. "I can't afford to make an enemy of him."

"You won't," said Chris confidently. "I don't think Herrera would ever accuse *you* of having a 'belligerent attitude'." The waitress gave us a look as she put down our order.

"Is that what he said? That you had a belligerent attitude?"

Chris grinned. "It was one of the more complimentary things." He winked. "I guess I'm not very good at bowing to power."

I could have told him that. Almost anybody at Red

Bay High could have told him that. "What else did he say?"

Chris scooped up an enormous spoonful of ice-cream. "Let's just say that Marva swore that if she got Herrera as her teacher she was going to change her last name so he wouldn't know we were related."

"Good grief," I said. "I guess he really doesn't like you."

The smile disappeared from Chris's face. "He likes me a lot more than I like him."

Even when he'd been screaming at me about scaring Geronimo his voice hadn't sounded that hard.

It seemed like a good time to go back to talking about me. "So, what do you think I should do?" I asked. "Bomb the lab?"

He laughed. "My idea's not quite that drastic."

Chris's idea was that I should picket the classroom on the day of the dissection. I should carry a sign and draw attention to myself. The way he described my protest made it sound as though I'd be striking a blow for academic freedom.

"Hey, I know," I said, getting carried away. "I could dress up as a frog. You know, to make people really notice me and get my point across!" As soon as I said it, I knew it was a dumb idea.

"What a great idea!" said Chris. "That's absolutely

brilliant. We could get Marva to help us with the costume. She's very artistic."

Us? This was getting out of hand. I was always having dumb ideas, but usually no one paid any attention to them. I stirred my milkshake with my straw. "I don't know about this," I said slowly. "Maybe I should just cut up the frog and forget about it."

"It's up to you," said Chris. It was the sort of thing my mother always said when she wanted you to know what she would do without actually coming out and telling you. "You should do what *you* want, but not just because you're worried about what anyone else is going to say or do." He paid our bill.

I didn't know how to explain that I wasn't like him and Marva, you know, weird and outspoken. I was going on a diet. I was becoming a natural blonde. I was toying with the idea of fitting in. "I'll think about it," I promised as we walked up Main Street.

"Passive resistance," said Chris. "Civil disobedience. Remember Ghandi. Remember Martin Luther King."

I remembered Amy. Civil disobedience was not what high school was about.

We turned off Main Street. Out of the corner of my eye I could see two familiar figures walking towards us on the other side of the street. At first I thought it was

Amy and Kim. Then I thought it was Rosie Henley and Amber. We were almost parallel. It was Amber and Kim. They pretended they didn't see us, but I saw them give each other a nudge.

"So I'll see you tomorrow?" Chris was saying.

I looked up at him. "What?"

"I'll see you tomorrow after school. We can talk some more about your demonstration, if you want." He grinned. "Or I can introduce you to my bats."

"OK," I said, sort of answering automatically, "I'll see you then."

After I finished my homework that night, I locked myself in the bathroom to become a natural blonde. According to the instructions, all I had to do was apply a treatment every time I shampooed my hair, leave it for ten to fifteen minutes, rinse it out with warm water and, miracle of miracles, within a few weeks I would slowly and subtly become a real blonde.

I washed my hair. I opened the first silver envelope and thoroughly rubbed the contents into each strand, starting from the crown. It made me smell like the chemistry lab and look like I'd had an encounter of the third kind. While I waited for fifteen minutes to pass, I sat on the floor of the bathroom, reading up on Schrödinger from a book I'd gotten at the library after I left Chris. It was a pretty interesting book. It was so interesting that by the time I checked my watch again twenty-five minutes had passed. After I'd rinsed out the treatment, I studied myself in the mirror. My hair was still brown. It looked almost darker, if you want the truth. "It's because it works slowly and subtly," I reminded myself. "Like nature."

After that, I went to my room to study *The Ultimate Dieter*. As far as I could figure out, the ultimate dieter was a person who didn't eat. Or not much. The ultimate dieter didn't let her body trick her into wanting chocolate or French fries. The ultimate dieter taught herself to love the things that were good for her – carrots and seaweed and boiled chicken, for instance – and to hate lasagne and double-cheese pizza. She drank diet soda and black tea and coffee. She weighed everything before she put it in her mouth. She knew that if she ate one slice of crispbread more than she was allowed, she'd be sorry. I read over the calorie chart and the fat chart and the fibre chart and the carbohydrate chart at the back of the book. I discovered the answer to my question at lunch the other day: how many calories are there in a tiny, infinitesimal piece of chocolate cake? Six hundred and thirty-eight! I nearly fainted. I collapsed on my bed. I didn't have the nerve to look up milkshake. It was scary. Everything was out to get me. I shut the book with a sigh.

It looked like I was going to be waging open warfare on more than Mr Herrera in the weeks ahead. It looked like I was declaring war on myself.

Not only was my hair as brown as ever when I woke up on Thursday, but by the end of school I was so hungry that depression was setting in. How was I going to get through the rest of the day – never mind the rest of the week – when all I could think about was food?

And then I saw them, standing in front of the library. At first I thought I must be hallucinating. There were two figures waiting for someone at the end of the path. One figure was tall and gaunt and all in black; the other was smaller and heavier and wearing a long purple dress, a purple scarf wound through her hair, and a silver and purple shawl. With all the kids hurrying past in their jeans and trainers, it was like coming upon visitors from another galaxy in the supermarket.

It's lack of carbohydrates, I told myself. *That's all it is, a carbohydrate deficiency.* And then I realized that the figures were waving to me. *Good grief*, I thought, *it's Chris and Marva*. I'd never seen the two of them together in daylight before. Not only were they waving to me, but I finally realized it was me they were waiting for. Between worrying about my hair and my lack of essential nutrients, I'd forgotten all about going back to their house this afternoon to plan my protest. I walked a little faster. Maybe it was just because they'd take my mind off pizza, but I was really glad to see them.

"Dig this," said Marva as I came up to them. "He's actually going to be seen with me in public." She made a face and nodded towards her brother. "The last time Chris walked home with me I was in fourth grade."

Chris made a face back. "I'm not walking home with you now," he said, falling into step beside me. "I'm walking home with frog girl."

I laughed. All of a sudden being called "frog girl" by Chris didn't seem like such an awful thing.

Marva winked at me. "Frog girl and bat boy," she said. "What a pair!" Her long skirt swooshing, her shawl flapping and her bracelets jangling, Marva fell into step on my other side.

Chris grabbed my arm. "You'll never guess what I found in the attic last night." He sounded really excited.

"Is it black and hanging upside down?" I guessed.

Chris laughed. "No, it's my old telescope. It used to be my grandfather's so it isn't exactly modern, but it's pretty good. I thought we could fix it up for you. Till you get your own."

I couldn't hide my surprise. I'd mentioned in passing that I was saving up for a telescope, but the one that I wanted was so expensive I'd be lucky to have enough for it by the time I left high school, and here he was offering me one.

"Oh, don't start talking about planets," said Marva in a bored voice. "Tell Jenny about the time Herrera tried to embarrass you in front of the whole school."

Chris grinned, but it wasn't exactly a happy grin. It suddenly occurred to me that though I wouldn't want to make an enemy of Mr Herrera, I wouldn't want to make an enemy of Chris County either.

"Which time?" he asked coldly. "Humiliating me is practically his hobby."

Marva reached across me and gave him a slap. "You know," she said. "The time he was giving you that special award, and when you went up to get it he took one look at what you were wearing and asked if you were trying to be as peculiar as possible."

I was horrified. "Good grief," I gasped. "What were you wearing?"

Marva sounded a lot like a whooping crane when she was really laughing. "His endangered species coat!" she whooped.

"Marva painted my old raincoat with animals like

dolphins, elephants and jaguars," Chris explained. "Since the award was for a paper I'd written on eagles, I thought it was appropriate to the occasion."

I tried to imagine what I'd say if Mr Herrera asked me in front of the school if I were trying to be as peculiar as possible. I figured I'd faint. "But what did you *do*?"

Chris grinned again, but this time with humour. "I said yes. I said that if it brought attention to the way we treated other species, then it was worth it." He did a little dance. "The audience gave me a standing ovation!"

The three of us were still laughing as we left the school ground. There were a lot of kids on the sidewalk, talking and just hanging out. It was then that I noticed three curly blonde heads looking in our direction. I couldn't decide whether I should nod or wave or something, you know, just to acknowledge the fact that I'd seen Amy. I mean, technically, she was still my best friend. But before I could do anything the heads turned away.

Dawn gets lost

My mother likes to tell me that "it's always darkest before the dawn". Whenever I get depressed or it seems like nothing in my life is going right, my mother will say, "Don't forget, honey, it's always darkest before the dawn."

By the end of my second week of self-improvement, I felt like I must be in the Land of Endless Night or something. How much darkness was I supposed to put up with? Where was this stupid dawn?

Being an ultimate dieter was like being trapped in a black hole. It was just about driving me out of my mind. I was sick of measuring everything, and weighing everything, and counting every single thing I put in my mouth. According to *The Ultimate Dieter*, if every day I ate one teaspoon of hamburger relish over the numbers of calories my body needed to maintain itself, I'd gain thirty pounds in the next ten years! Thirty pounds just for a teaspoon of hamburger relish! Now I understood why Amy's mother was always on a diet. What choice did she have if just one teaspoon of hamburger relish too many could turn you into a blimp? How did she stand it? When did it end? I wondered if I would have to have my lips glued together.

When I closed my eyes at night, I saw a pair of scales floating in the dark. When I dreamt, I dreamt of bowls of spaghetti and platters of grilled cheese sandwiches with tomato and onion and pickle on the side. When I woke up, I woke up hungry. I was hungry all day long. I admit I had always been the sort of person who thinks about what she's having for supper while she's rating lunch, but I hadn't been obsessive. I just ate a lot. And often. Now I ate a little and almost never. But I thought about food all the time. I thought about food when I was eating my three-hundred-calorie meals. I thought about food on the way to school and back again. I thought about food in every class. I nearly passed out in Spanish when the Riveras, the family in our textbook, stopped at a country inn for dinner and Senora Rivera ordered sausages and potato salad. I got hit in the head by the volleyball in gym because instead of paying attention to the other team I was thinking about a chicken burrito.

I couldn't watch television because of the ads. Soup, salad, cereal, waffles, pizza... How was a person supposed to be thin when she was always being told to eat? Sometimes after supper I'd just stand next to the refrigerator, with my head against the door, imagining the leftovers on the other side. "Eat me" they were shouting. "Eat me! Eat me! Just one bite!" I suggested to my mother that it might be a good idea to tape the door of the refrigerator shut. You know, just in case I started sleepwalking or something. There was an absolutely terrifying story in *The Ultimate Dieter* about a woman who gained fifty pounds in her sleep. Every night, she'd sleepwalk into her kitchen and eat peanut butter and jelly by the spoonful. In the morning she'd find empty jars and dirty utensils in the sink, and sometimes there'd even be crumbs, but she'd have no memory of eating anything at all.

My mother didn't believe in my diet. She thought I was being ridiculous. "I suppose we should be grateful you haven't decided that your nose is too big," she said, "or you'd be down in the basement, sawing it off."

And if that wasn't dark enough, the really tragic thing was that for all my suffering and agonizing, I wasn't losing any weight. In fact, somehow, as I discovered on the second Saturday after I started my diet, I'd gained a pound. How can you live on twelve hundred calories a day for nearly three whole weeks and *gain* a pound?

"Water," said my mother. "That's all it is. Just water."

"Water?" I repeated. "How can water weigh so much?"

"Trust me," said my mother. "It's water." But if all that wasn't dark enough, that same day my hair turned green.

I'd been putting the Natural Blonde in it every time I washed it, just like the instructions said, but nothing much happened. I guess I was too nervous – you know, in case my hair fell out or turned white or something and my parents grounded me for the rest of my life – so after that first time I never left it in for very long. If I stood in direct light you could see a few glints of gold among the muddy brown, but otherwise it looked exactly the same. I think I was kind of relieved. And then, I went swimming as usual on Saturday, and by the time I got home my hair was green.

The first clue I had was when I walked into the house, and my father sort of squinted at me and said, "Jenny, is your hair always that colour?"

I thought he must be working too hard or something. "*Brown?*" I asked.

"Not brown," said my father. "It looks kind of green."

I laughed. "I think you'd better have your glasses checked, Dad," I said. "My hair's not green. It's brown."

My mother came into the room. She stopped dead in the doorway. "Jenny Kaliski," said my mother, "what on earth have you done to your hair?"

"Nothing," I said.

"Nothing my frozen yoghurt," said my mother. Her voice went up an octave. "It's green!"

My father said it was probably a chemical reaction between the bleach I'd used and the chlorine in the pool. He said the best thing to do was just to let it grow out.

"Can't we dye it brown or something?" I begged my mother. It was green like grass or parsley, it was green like pond scum.

But my mother is a woman of principle. "Serves you right," she said, "putting that junk on your beautiful hair."

By Saturday night, I was pretty sure the dawn was never going to come. But then came Sunday and two tiny glimmers of light.

On Sunday afternoon Chris called to say that Marva had finished my frog costume and it was ready to try on. I wasn't quite sure how or when I'd agreed to this – but I had. There was something about Chris and Marva and their enthusiasm for everything they did that made all my objections seem small and petty. Marva was sitting on the front porch with the dog when I arrived. The first thing she said when she saw me was, "Jenny, why are you wearing a scarf? You look like a Russian peasant."

I marched up the stairs. "I'll show you when I'm inside."

"Wow!" said Marva when I took off the scarf. "That is wild! I wish I'd thought of that! What made you decide to dye your hair green?"

"Nothing," I said glumly. "I was trying to become a natural blonde."

Chris came into the hall with Geronimo on his shoulder. "What for?" he asked. "Your hair has all that red in it, it's much nicer than blonde." He raised his eyebrows. "Well, it used to have all that red in it."

"I think the green is great," said Marva. "It's very original. And appropriate for someone who's dressing up as a frog."

She picked up my scarf with two fingers. "Well, you can't go to school looking like a potato picker," she said.

Chris shrugged. "So cut it."

"Cut it?" I repeated.

"Of course! Cut it all off!" Marva clapped her hands. "He really is a genius, you know."

I wasn't so sure about this. My hair wasn't really long, but it wasn't really short either. "Cut it all off?" I asked again.

Marva grabbed my hand and started yanking me towards the bathroom. "Come on," she said. "Let's do it now before you change your mind!"

"What are you talking about?" I demanded. "I haven't said I'd do it yet."

"Of course you'll do it," said Marva. "It's better than spending the next six months wearing a turban."

Chris followed us. "Don't worry, Jen," he said from the doorway as Marva sat me down on a stool in the County's enormous old bathroom and threw a towel around my shoulders. "You've got the face for really short hair. It'll look great."

The funny thing was, it did look great, it really did. Marva said it made my eyes look bigger. And it was so short that you could hardly tell it wasn't brown.

"You see?" said Chris from behind me. It had been a long time since I'd worn any, but I was trying on some of Marva's silver hoops to see what the effect of three earrings in my right ear would be with my new haircut. It was OK. Chris smiled at me in the mirror. "What'd I tell you? You look terrific."

Marva put her head on my shoulder. "Chris is right," she said. "It's very *you*."

Then on Saturday night, Amy Ford called me up.

"I thought maybe you'd want to walk to school together tomorrow," she said.

"Me?"

"I really miss you, Jen," said Amy quietly. "Remember

when we used to go to school together every day?"

"Yeah," I said, hiding my surprise and playing it cool, "I have a vague recollection."

Amy laughed. "That's what I miss the most," she said. "Your sense of humour."

To tell you the truth, I was more than surprised by Amy's call. I was shocked. Staggered. Knocked over the head with a ten-pound salami. I mean, you tell someone all her major flaws, you pretty much stop speaking to her except for an occasional "Hi, there!" or "Hello!" when you pass in the hall, and then you suddenly call her up and ask to see her. Not only to see her, but to be seen walking into school with her. Why? That's what I kept asking myself after she hung up. Why? I'd been doing my Spanish homework and thinking about fried potatoes with gravy, but after her phone call all I could think of was Amy. Whywhywhywhywhy? *Because she misses you*, I told myself. *That's why. That's what she said. She misses you and your great sense of humour.*

To tell the truth, I'd forgotten about Amy over the last couple of weeks. To begin with, I was seeing a lot of Chris and Marva. After that Thursday when I went home with them, it was just sort of taken for granted that we'd all walk to and from school together. Most afternoons I'd go back to their house, and Chris and I would work on the telescope while Marva sat near us, reading out loud. Or I'd bring over one of my dad's nature videos and the three of us, and Geronimo, would watch it together. Chris really admired my dad's collection.

But besides that, I'd been spending more time with the rest of the Martians, too. We had more in common than I'd thought. We liked a lot of the same things, and we found a lot of the same things funny. Maria was helping me with my Spanish, and it turned out that Joan's great passion was planets. "Plants, planets, bats," Marva liked to grumble. "I don't understand why I'm surrounded by all you science types. It makes me nuts." In fact, except that I was starving, I was having an OK time. One day after school the six of us had gone to the mall, and Tanya had us all in stitches, trying on clothes. The Saturday before, we'd all gone to a movie, and Sue cracked us up by shouting out instructions to the heroine whenever she was about to get into trouble. "Don't trust him!" Sue yelled. "Oh, no, don't go in there!" I thought I was going to choke I was laughing so much.

After Amy's phone call, though, I started thinking about her again. I thought of all the things we used to do together, and how close we'd been. And how sometimes, when I caught a glimpse of her across the campus or down the corridor with one of her new friends, my heart would sort of flop.

And then, as I lay on my bed thinking, I understood why Amy had suddenly started missing me. It was because she'd noticed me with the Martians. Maybe she'd even seen me in town with Marva, or at the library with Joan, or at the mall on Saturday with everyone. I knew she'd seen me with Marva and Chris. She'd seen me with them, and she wished we were best friends again. Maybe she'd seen me and Tanya fooling around, and she'd thought to herself, *That used to be me!*, just the way I did when I saw her giggling with Amber and Kim.

I couldn't help smiling to myself as I got into bed and turned off the light. *Jenny Kaliski*, I said to myself, *you're about to hit dawn!*

"Jenny Kaliski," said my mother, "just where do you think you're going?"

I stopped at the front door. It was Monday morning. I was wearing one of my best pairs of jeans, a black shirt, my denim jacket and two silver hoops and a silver bat earring that Chris had given me because he had a pair and he wore only one. I had my book bag over my shoulder and a paper bag with my lunch in it in my hand. Where did she think I was going?

"School?"

"Without any breakfast?"

"I don't have time for breakfast, Mom. I'll be late."

She formed her lips into a straight line. "I don't care if you're on a diet or not," said my mother. "You have to eat."

"It's not the diet, Mom, honest," I said. "I just don't want to be late for school."

My mother said, "Um."

I sprinted through the door before my mother could think of anything else to say. It was true, I didn't want to be late that morning. Dawn was breaking. I was meeting Amy. I was meeting Amy and she was going to tell me how sorry she was for all the awful things she'd said about me and for treating me so badly and we were going to be friends again. That's what I was thinking as I hurried down the street. Amy was going to apologize and we'd still be friends.

"Jenny! Jenny, wait up!"

I turned around, Amy was cutting across the Carlotti's front yard, running towards me, her hair glinting in the sun. I'd been so lost in thought that I'd gone past her street. Seeing Amy jump over the Carlotti's miniature picket fence and the stone pig in the middle of the lawn, like she always did, was kind of strange. I felt like I was watching a video of my life. "Jenny Kaliski!" boomed a voice in my head. "Jenny Kaliski, this is your life! And here is your best friend since third grade, Amy Ford, racing to meet you on a Monday morning." Only it wasn't a video, it was the real thing. I felt such a rush of happiness that for a minute there I even forgot I was hungry.

"Whew," Amy laughed, falling into step beside me, "I was afraid I might've missed you."

And that was when I realized that only half of me was happy. The other half had an attitude. The half with the attitude felt like saying, *You did miss me. You missed me yesterday, and the day before that, and the day before that ...* but I shut that half up. The happy half of me didn't want to fight with Amy, it wanted to be friends. So I laughed, too, and said, "Is your hair lighter, or is there something wrong with my eyes?"

"Do you like it? Kim did it."

I thought it was a familiar shade. "It's nice," I said. "It's very blonde."

"Nordic gold," said Amy. She was so close to me that our arms touched. "Gosh," she said, smiling, "it seems like ages since I've talked to you."

I smiled, too. "Thirteen days."

"There's that famous sense of humour again!" laughed Amy. She gave me a wink. And then she said, "You know, you look different, somehow." She gave me another wink. "I mean, besides the hair. I don't know how you ever had the nerve to cut it so short. *Nobody* wears their hair that short any more." She tilted her head to one side and frowned. "I wonder what it is…"

I didn't say that everyone else, even my parents, thought my hair looked great, I suppose because I was so grateful that she hadn't noticed it was green. But also because what I really wanted was for her to say I looked thinner. "Why, Jen!" I wanted her to say. "I know what it is! You're skinny! You must've lost pounds. You look absolutely gorgeous!" I *willed* her to say it.

"You haven't put on a little weight, have you?" she asked.

Terrific. Amy was getting blonder and blonder, and I was getting fatter and greener. Probably I was getting shorter, too. "No," I said loudly. "I haven't put on weight." One pound didn't count.

She tilted her head to the other side. "Maybe it's the earrings," she said. "You've started wearing three earrings again."

Even my father thought the earrings looked good with my new haircut. Distinctive was what he'd said. I could tell from Amy's expression that she didn't agree with my father. As far as she was concerned, this wasn't the right thing to do either. "Yeah, well, you know…" I started to explain. "You know, I figured since the holes were there already—"

"Maybe it *is* your hair," she interrupted, peering. "It looks darker or something."

I decided to change the subject. "Well, you look really great," I said brightly. She did, too. She looked like one of the girls in my magazine. The girls who didn't have cellulite. I looked at her again. "Your eyes even look bluer."

She smiled. "Tinted lenses. All the girls have them."

"Oh, right," I said. "Of course."

We scuffed along through the leaves in silence for a few minutes. This wasn't exactly the reunion I'd imagined. Amy and I had been friends for eight years, and here I was walking along with her and I couldn't think of a thing to say. She wouldn't be interested in hearing about the telescope. She'd make fun of me if I told her the truth about my hair. She'd be horrified if I told her about my protest. She'd think the things that the Martians and I did and laughed about were dumb or immature. Dawn started fading again.

And then, in a sudden rush, Amy said, "So, Jenny, what have you been up to lately?"

I concentrated on kicking a horse chestnut into the road. There was something about her voice that didn't really sound natural. I wasn't sure why, but it made me sort of suspicious,

I shrugged. "Oh, nothing much," I said. "I go to

school and that's about it. You know, the usual. What about you?"

"Oh, the same," said Amy. "I mean, I have cheerleading, that keeps me pretty busy, and there've been a lot of other things going on lately, social things, you know, and of course Rosie Henley's Hallowe'en party is coming up and I've been working on my costume for that. Did I tell you that I decided to go as a mermaid?"

When do you think you told me? the half of me with attitude wanted to say. *In your sleep?* But the other half was still in control. "Everyone misses you at swimming," I said as we turned towards the school.

"Swimming?" She gave me this sort of blank look. "You mean you still go swimming?"

I nodded. "Of course I still go swimming." Not only did I like swimming but *The Ultimate Dieter* had recommended it for exercise.

"But it makes your calves so thick." She gave me a little shiver. "Not to mention what it does to your arms."

"Oh," I mumbled. I was glad I was wearing my jacket, so neither of us could check to see what swimming had done to my arms.

We crossed the street.

"So," said Amy, as we started up the drive, "I hear you're hanging out with Chris County now."

She sounded so offhand that all at once I knew that this was it. This was what she'd been leading to. Miss me, my frozen yoghurt, as my mother would say. Chris County, not missing me, was the reason Amy wanted to walk to school with me.

"Not exactly hanging out." I kept my eyes straight ahead. "I'm friends with his sister."

"Oh, his *sister*," groaned Amy. "She's peculiar, too." She tossed her head. "But all those girls you hang out with are a little weird."

So she *had* noticed. It just hadn't broken her heart that I was with Marva, Maria, Joan, Sue and Tanya instead of her. She leaned closer to me. "Do you know what everyone calls them?" She giggled nervously.

I didn't want to know. I mean, I knew they were Martians and everything, but for some reason I didn't want to hear what name Amy and her crowd had for them. Only I didn't say that to Amy. To Amy I said, "Everybody?"

"Well, not *me*," she said quickly. "I don't call them this, but others do." She gave another nervous giggle. "The Witches of Red Bay!" she said. She was smiling at me as though her face had frozen. "It *is* kind of funny, isn't it? The Witches of Red Bay! Couldn't you just *die*?"

Yeah, I thought, *I think I could*. I wondered if she'd noticed that one of my earrings was a bat.

Amy abruptly stopped smiling. "They're harmless, of course," she continued. "I mean, hanging out with them isn't going to *help* your social life any, but it shouldn't do you any permanent damage. I mean, if you ever decided to dump them and get in with the right people, everyone would probably forget that you ever knew them at all. At least they'd forgive you."

Forgive me? Now there was a piece of good news. Things were definitely looking up. Maybe dawn was breaking after all. "Amy," I began, "I have no intention—"

She cut me off. "But Christopher County is different," she said sharply. "He is too weird for words."

I'm not sure what it was, but something in the way she said "too weird for words" made me think she'd rehearsed whatever I was about to hear. I glanced over at her. Her mouth was set and she was staring straight ahead. "He's not that weird," I said. "He happens to be very nice. He's—"

"Weird," repeated Amy. "He's as weird as they come. He's never done one normal thing during his whole high school career. He's arrogant and antisocial. He gives everyone the creeps."

"He doesn't give me the creeps," I said. "I think he's really interesting. And anyway, he's helping me with my protest." As soon as the words were out of my mouth I

remembered that I hadn't been going to mention the protest to Amy. As soon as I saw the expression on her face, I knew I'd been right.

She was so surprised that she looked at me. "Helping you with what protest?"

I tried to sound matter-of-fact. "Remember I told you about Mr Herrera and the frogs?"

"What frogs?" asked Amy.

"You know," I said. "I told you about Mr Herrera insisting that I dissect a frog." I was trying to keep my voice normal, but I was having a little trouble. Because by then her surprise had been replaced by something else. By horror. I looked away. "Well, I decided to stage a protest instead."

She didn't say anything, but I could feel her staring at me.

"You know," I said, talking quickly. "Like Ghandi and Martin Luther King."

Amy came to a dead stop, but she still didn't say anything. And because she didn't say anything, I started to babble.

"I'm going to picket the dissection lab," I told her. "I'm going to dress up like a frog and I'm going to march outside the classroom with a sign."

"You're kidding, right?" Her voice, now that she'd found it, was completely flat.

I shook my head, picking up more speed. "No, I'm not kidding. I'm going to stand up for my principles. I'm going to strike a blow for academic freedom. I'm going to—"

"Humiliate yourself in front of the entire school." While I'd babbled, the expression of horror on Amy's face had changed from basic horror to horrified horror. "I can't believe you're doing this." She was almost whispering. "I really can't believe it. Have you lost your mind, Jenny? Don't you care at all what other people think? Are you trying to be as weird as you can?"

"No," I said. "I'm not trying to be weird. I'm trying to stand up for what I believe."

All of a sudden she smiled. "This is Chris County's idea, isn't it?" It was a triumphant smile. "You're letting Chris County put ideas in your head." She made a disgusted face. "And I thought you were smart. How can you listen to anything a nut like Chris has to say?" She started walking again. "Well, at least this explains why he's hanging out with *you*."

The way she said "you" made me sound like an earthworm. *Well at least that explains why he's hanging out with an earthworm.*

"And what's that supposed to mean?" I had run a few steps to catch up with her. "One minute you're telling me how weird he is, and the next you're acting like I'm not good enough for him."

"Oh, don't be ridiculous." Amy strode on. "All I meant was that you're obviously gullible enough to take him seriously."

If she hadn't wounded my pride, I might have pointed out that most of the teachers at school took Chris seriously. But she had wounded my pride, so what I said was, "Maybe he likes me, Amy. Did you ever think of that? Maybe he likes being with me."

"Oh, please," said my oldest friend. "Chris County looks down on *everybody*. He hangs out with no one." She shook her Nordic curls. "Can you believe it? Rosie Henley invited him to a party once and he turned her down flat! Rosie Henley! Who does he think he is?"

Talk about weird… This strange idea suddenly came into my head. *Good grief*, I thought. *Could it be that they're jealous? Could it be that the Miss Perfect Teenagers are mad because Chris County hangs out with me but won't speak to them?*

Amy gave me another one of her frozen smiles. "But I guess if you're dumb enough to go along with him…"

"I am not dumb enough to go along with him," I protested. "It just so happens that Chris likes—"

"To cause trouble," filled in Amy. "Especially where Mr Herrera's concerned, from what I've heard." She sighed.

"You're too trusting, Jenny. But I can tell you right now that Chris County is just using you. If he's helping you it's for himself, not for you. That's the way people like him are."

Using me? I repeated to myself. *Using me for what?* It was starting to annoy me that she wouldn't listen to anything I said. "Chris is—"

"Bad news," said Amy. "Serious bad news. Don't you know that he's always in trouble? Didn't you hear how he nearly got kicked out of school?"

We were no longer walking, we were marching.

Amy means he's using you to get back at Mr Herrera. I pushed the thought out of my head. "No, he's not," I said. "He happens to be one of the smartest people—"

"He's a pariah," snapped Amy.

"A *pariah?*" Where had she gotten that word from? *Pariah* was not an Amy Ford word.

She shook the golden head. "Being friends with him could ruin your life."

I couldn't get over her. You'd think she was an elephant warning another elephant about the ivory traders. "Ruin my life? What are you talking about? How could knowing Chris ruin my life?"

Amy swung her book bag as we marched across the quad. "People are judged by their friends."

"That's funny," I said. "I thought they were judged by

their clothes and their hair and how much they weighed."

She wasn't listening to that either. "No one likes him, Jenny," she said with finality. "If they don't like him, they won't like you."

"That's not true. Lots of people like him. He has—"

"Rosie Henley doesn't like him," said Amy evenly. "And neither does Dwayne Miller."

And Mr Herrera doesn't like him. I told myself to shut up. "So what? He probably doesn't like them."

She stopped dead. She turned to face me. "So what? Jenny, don't you realize that hanging out with Chris County is committing social suicide? I was even going to try and get you an invitation to Rosie's Hallowe'en party, but there's no way I could do that now…"

"So what?" I said. "I don't care."

This genuinely pained expression came into her eyes. "How can you?" she asked. "How can you not care?"

"I just don't," I said. "I—"

"Well, maybe you don't care now," said Amy. "But what if you decide later that you do care? Chris County will be graduating in June, but you won't. You'll be here for another three years. What if you change your mind? What if you realize what a mistake you've made? Do you think that anyone will give you the time of day once they know you're a friend of *his*?"

"They don't give me the time of day now," I reasoned.

"But they would," said Amy earnestly. She sounded as if she believed it. "They would if you'd make an effort, I know they would." She moved a little closer, her voice an urgent whisper. "I really worry about you, Jenny. I know you don't think I do, but I do. I never dreamed we'd drift apart like this. I thought we'd always be close. Remember when your mom used to say we were like two peas in a pod? What happened, Jenny?"

I couldn't answer. I didn't know.

We started walking again, but slowly, side by side, our shoulders almost touching.

"I don't want you to be an outcast," she said softly. "I want you to belong. Like I do."

"But, Amy—"

"I knew everything would be different in high school," she was saying, "but not like this…"

We came to a sudden halt outside the entrance that led directly to Amy's locker. Amy turned to me. For the first time in weeks it was the old Amy I was seeing. The Amy who loved me. The Amy who was a pea in my pod. "I can't stand to see you ruining your life like this," said Amy. Her voice shook. "When I think of what good friends we were…" She trailed off, her eyes on the ground. "I just really can't," she whispered.

I opened my mouth, sort of to see if I could speak or not, but Amy was already stepping into the hall. The door banged shut behind her. One of those silly rhymes people write in your yearbook popped into my head as I watched her disappear into the building. Only it was a little different than it usually is. "There are gold ships and there are silver ships," I recited to myself, "but the sinking ship is friendship."

"What's the matter?" asked Tanya through a mouthful of chicken salad. "You seem a little down."

I looked over at her. Tanya always talked while she ate, so either you couldn't understand what she was saying or there were bits of food falling out of her mouth while you were trying to have a discussion with her. Usually it didn't bother me, but today I thought it was gross. "Do you have to talk and eat at the same time?" I snapped.

"Ooooh!" screeched Tanya, rolling her eyes and pretending to pull away from me. "Not only down, but touchy, too."

"Yuk yuk yuk," I said.

Tanya was right, though, I was down. And I was touchy, too. At first I'd thought that Amy was just being mean and awful to me because she didn't like me any more. But now I knew that she did like me. She liked me and she was as upset as I was about the way things had turned out. I kept seeing the look on her face as we stood outside the school. She really was worried about me. She really cared.

And that was why I'd been silent all through lunch. I'd been watching the Martians through Amy's eyes. Everything about them was annoying me. The way they looked. The way they spoke. The way they ate. Marva's opinions. Joan's patience. Maria's sweetness. The fact that Sue was always two conversations behind everyone else. How had I let myself get so involved with them? Amy was right. They were oddballs. They were more than oddballs. They were the oddest of oddballs.

"So?" Tanya persisted. "What's eating you?"

I looked away as a piece of lettuce drifted onto her blouse. "It's nothing," I lied. "I guess I'm just a little tired, that's all."

"It's your stupid diet," said Marva in her loud, grating voice. How could someone with purple hair and half a dozen earrings sound so much like my mom? "You're not getting the right nutrition, so you've got no energy."

"Oh, give it a rest, will you, Marv?" said Joan. She leaned towards me, holding out an apple. "Why don't you take this? You've hardly eaten a thing."

I held up my hand. "Really, Joan," I said, trying not to

lose my temper, "I'm not hungry." That at least was true. If Mr Salteri, owner of Pizza Passion, had walked into the cafeteria right then and offered me a free meal at his restaurant, all I could eat plus a doggie bag, I would have said, "No, thank you, Mr Salteri. I don't feel like pizza or lasagne right now."

"How about a brownie?" asked Sue.

"No," I repeated. "Really ... I'm fine."

Maria put her hand on my forehead. "I hope you're not coming down with something," she said.

I pushed her away. "What are you guys?" I snapped. "My mothers?"

Tanya bounced a balled-up sandwich bag off my head. "No," she said, "we're your friends."

That afternoon, mainly because I couldn't think of any way to get out of it, I went over to Marva's to put the finishing touches to my frog costume. The dissection was scheduled for next Wednesday. D-day, as Chris called it.

"Well, what do you think?" asked Chris. He was standing behind me, grinning as I stared into the mirror.

I was looking at myself through Amy's eyes. I looked ridiculous. I looked like a girl who would never fit in. I looked like a girl who was gullible enough to go along with a crazy scheme that would humiliate her in front of the entire school.

"I don't know," I said slowly, "maybe this isn't such a good idea after all."

Chris put an arm around me. I had to admit it. He was weird. He was wearing a black turtle neck and baggy old sweat pants, and his hair was hanging loose to his shoulders except for a couple of tiny braids. Forget about not looking like any other boy in the school, he didn't look like any other boy in the state.

"Don't be silly," he said. "It's a great idea. Dignity and dissent! King and Ghandi would be proud of you!"

I stared at his reflection. He looked really pleased. I couldn't help wondering if he looked really pleased because he was proud of me, too, or if it was because there was no one else in Red Bay gullible enough to be talked into dressing up like a frog. Because he'd been waiting for three years to get even with Mr Herrera and I was his last chance.

Chris gave me a squeeze, leaning his head close to mine. "And besides," he said, "you look terrific. Green's really your colour."

Marva, who was in one corner of the room, practising her yoga, began reciting another of her poems. "'*I'm no-body...*'" she boomed. "'*Are you nobody, too? ... How dreadful to be somebody, how public, like a frog...*'"

The best thing you could say was that I definitely looked like a frog. A short, slightly pudgy frog. I was wearing the one-piece green jumpsuit and papier-mâché hood that covered my hair, my ears and my forehead. The whole thing had been hand-painted to look realistic enough to suit Chris, which meant realistic enough to suit another frog. And I was going to be a public frog, that was for sure. Amy's voice whispered in my mind. *Humiliate yourself in front of the entire school*, it was saying. *Have you lost your mind?* it was asking. *Don't you care at all what other people think? Are you trying to be as weird as you can?* I couldn't take my eyes off myself. Everyone in the school was going to see me in this stupid costume. Here I was, not wanting to be the centre of attention and I was planning to walk in front of the science building with a sign that said: *All Creatures Have Rights! End Unnecessary Experimentation Now!* I stared at my large webbed hands. And started thinking about what was the difference between standing up for your beliefs and looking like a fool.

"Not only am I going to do a piece for the school paper on you," Chris went on, "but I think they're going to let me do one for the town paper, too. Isn't that great?"

Marva looked over from the corner. "With a picture," she informed me happily.

"Great," I said. "I can't wait."

Chris winked at me in the mirror. "Herrera's going to be sorry he wouldn't listen to reason."

I couldn't help wondering if I was going to be sorry I wouldn't listen to reason, too.

I turn yellow not blonde

In August I'd tried to get my mother to let me stay up all night to watch some meteor showers. My mother said no. She'd said I was a growing girl and needed rest. I'd said I was fourteen and almost an adult. My mother'd said that being an adult wasn't about how late you were allowed to stay up. She'd said it was how you dealt with problems and crises and difficult situations.

"You mean like the way Dad always goes camping when Grandma and Grandpa come to stay?" I'd asked.

"Don't be a wise guy, Jenny," my mother had said. "You know exactly what I mean. Being an adult is about how you handle yourself in the worst of times."

I was in the worst of times. My oldest friend was worried about me. She was afraid that I was ruining my life. She was concerned that I was gullible, that I was making the wrong choices. She knew me better than anyone except my parents, and she was really worried. And I was beginning to be worried, too. What was I doing? What had happened to shy, quiet, low-profile Jenny Kaliski, serious student and future astrophysicist? Here I was, about to go public as a frog and not only probably ruin my brilliant career as a scientist, but totally destroy my social life in high school for ever. I didn't know what I wanted any more. I had thought I wanted to be me. But who was *me*? What was *me*? How could *me* stand in front of the whole school dressed as Kermit?

I knew that this was just the sort of difficult situation that called for maturity and wisdom. I knew that this was exactly the sort of problem that demanded reason and logic. So I panicked.

I got home from Chris and Marva's that night and went straight to my room. My head hurt, my stomach ached, and I was hot enough to ignite. I took my old teddy bear, Bert, from the shelf, and lay on the bed with him. I cried for a while, but it didn't make me feel any better. It irritated my contacts so I had to take them out. I took them out and then I cried some more. "What am I going to do?" I finally asked Bert. "I don't think I can go through with this."

Bert stared back at me with his one plastic eye. I knew

what he was thinking. *Don't do it*, he was thinking. *Don't humiliate yourself in front of the whole school.*

"But what about my principles?" I asked him. "Chris is right, it's important to stand up for what I believe." I snuffled back a couple hundred tears.

Bert frowned. *Are you sure you're standing up for what you believe?* he wanted to know. *Are you sure you're not just fighting Chris's battle with Mr Herrera for him?*

"Of course I'm sure," I told him. "Chris couldn't be using me."

No? said Bert.

"No. He wouldn't. He likes me."

Because you're gullible, said Bert.

"No, because we have similar interests. And besides, it was my idea not to dissect the frog in the first place, not Chris's."

Bert's one eye shone. *But it was Chris's idea to picket the class. It's Chris who's encouraged you to make a public spectacle of yourself.*

He was right. It was Chris's idea. But he wasn't trying to manipulate me. He was trying to help me. "So I could strike a blow for academic freedom," I reminded Bert.

Bert twitched an ear. *You mean so Chris County could strike a blow against Mr Herrera.*

"That's not true," I said. It was amazing how much

like Amy Bert sounded. "It was so that even if I have to bow to power I could do it with dignity."

In a frog costume? asked Bert.

"Oh, good grief," I groaned. For two entire minutes, I'd forgotten about that. And to think, it was the one part of my protest that I'd come up with all by myself. "How can I do it? I'll be the laughing stock of the school. Unless, of course, Mr Herrera has me kicked out." That was the bright side. That Mr Herrera would get me kicked out of school and I would never have to show my face at Red Bay High again. Talk about dawn.

So don't, said Burt. *Just tell Chris you've changed your mind.*

"Tell Chris I've changed my mind?" I couldn't do that either. I couldn't look him in the eye and say that I didn't care how many frogs got cut up for nothing. I couldn't tell him that I didn't give a potato chip for Mars, he could fix up his telescope by himself. I just couldn't.

Back and forth I went. Back and forth, back and forth. *Life is not a bowl of cherries*, I told myself. *It's a see-saw.* Even my three-hundred-calorie supper couldn't lure me out of my room that night. When Chris called I told my mother to tell him I was taking a bath. When Marva called I told my mother to tell her I was asleep. But by the time I really was drifting off to sleep, I knew what I wanted to do. I wanted to stay in bed. Possibly for ever.

* * *

I figured I must be having some sort of mini nervous breakdown from all the pressure I was under. Only I didn't say that to my mother, of course. It wasn't the sort of thing she'd accept. Headaches, measles, colds, viruses, strained muscles and earaches, those were the things my mother understood. But not breakdowns. If I said, "Mom, I really don't feel very well, I'm under too much stress," she'd say, "Jenny, if you'd like to see what fifteen is like, I suggest you get your books and go to school. Now." So I told my mother I thought I had the flu. The symptoms were the same.

My mother felt my forehead.

"Everything aches," I moaned.

"You do feel warm," said my mother. "And you look flushed."

"My throat hurts, too."

"You'd better stay in bed," said my mother.

"If you insist." I sighed.

"I insist," said my mother. "Do you think you're well enough to be left alone while I go to work?"

"Do we have any juice?"

After my mother went to work, I lay on the couch, half-asleep and half-awake. Maybe I was delirious from the fever. Faces kept drifting in and out of my mind. Amy. Chris. Marva. Tanya. Kim. Amber. Rosie Henley. Sue. Maria. Mr Herrera. Frogs. If I could get away from school for a while, I remember thinking, the Martians would forget about me. When I finally went back, I just wouldn't go back to their table and they probably wouldn't even notice. I'd be thinner, because I would have lost so much weight during my illness, and I'd buy a pair of stretch jeans and a pair of cowboy boots like the popular girls wore. Amy would see that I had changed my mind, and she'd get Rosie Henley to invite me to her Hallowe'en party after all. I'd go as a cheerleader. I'd wear high-heeled sneakers and a blonde wig. I'd look so sensational in my costume that no one would realize it was me. The girls would all want to be friends with me and the boys would all want to ask me out. I woke up when Percy dropped his doggy bone on my chest.

What I wanted, I guess, was for everything and everyone to just go away. *Just go away*, I thought as I shuffled into the kitchen for something to drink. *That's all I ask. Just disappear.* In my weakened condition, I had the idea that if I left my problems at home, they would just straighten themselves out. Just as long as I didn't think about them. Sort of like how Fleming discovered penicillin. All he did was forget to wash the Petri dish. I was going to leave my dirty dishes in the sink for a few days and see what happened. If I was lucky, I figured, they would just disappear. I wouldn't really have to do one thing or another. It would be done for me. All I had to do was stay at home.

So I stayed at home. I just lay in bed, sleeping, reading and watching television – and trying not to think about my problems at all.

It started to work. As I sipped my juice and petted my dog, and ate grapes and crackers, and watched old movies, I found myself wondering what I'd been so worried and confused about. I felt exactly as I always had, like Jenny Kaliski, friend of animals, fan of the cosmos, a girl who liked nothing better than to lie in bed, eating and watching TV. I felt fine. By Tuesday afternoon, when my mother got home, not only was I feeling better, it really *was* like the rest of the world had gone away.

But not everyone stayed away.

Tuesday night, Marva and Joan both called to see why I hadn't been in school.

"If you're going to be out for a couple of days, I can bring you your homework," said Joan.

"Thanks," I said, "but I'm not going to be home that long."

"Chris says hi and he hopes you don't feel too awful," said Marva.

"Thanks," I said. "Tell him hi back."

I was still too sick to go to school on Wednesday morning. "Maybe a little French toast would make me feel better," I said to my mother.

My mother made me French toast, and then she made me fruit salad so I'd have something for later. I ate it while I read the magazines my father had brought me. They weren't like the magazines I'd bought in the drugstore. They were about things like dinosaurs, leatherback turtles and solar eclipses. I couldn't put them down.

Wednesday night, Marva, Maria and Tanya all called.

Tanya told me fourteen knock-knock jokes in a row, until I was laughing so much I couldn't breathe. They were really dumb.

Maria offered to pick up my homework for me.

"Thanks," I said, "but I'll probably be back tomorrow."

Marva told me some long story about an English actor who was in this big production, and even though he had the flu he went on, and then he died on stage.

"Are you trying to cheer me up?" I asked.

"Chris says to tell you that he's got the telescope ready," said Marva. "If you want he could bring it over so you could use it while you're sick."

"Tell him thanks," I said. "But I really don't feel up to it."

Thursday morning, my fever was gone, but I was still

feeling weak. "I wouldn't want to have a relapse," I told my mother.

My mother said she wouldn't want that either.

Thursday evening, Maria, Tanya and Sue stopped by. Maria brought me my homework. Tanya came to sing me a get well song. Sue had a book on comets she'd thought I might like.

"What nice girls," my mother said after they'd left. "Why don't you ever invite them over?"

I don't have to invite them, I thought. *They come over anyway.*

Out loud I said, "Really? You don't think they're a little odd?"

"Odd?" my mother repeated.

Hadn't she noticed that Tanya was built like a tank? That Maria didn't talk in front of her? That Sue never talked about what anyone else was talking about?

"Yeah," I said, "odd. You know, not like normal teenagers."

"They seem normal enough to me," said my mother.

On Friday my mother said she didn't see any reason for me to go to school, since I'd already missed most of the week. "Why take chances?" she asked.

I couldn't have agreed more. Even though I was feeling fine. Better than fine, really. I was feeling great. I was happy as a bat in a belfry. The happiest I'd been in ages. I guess I'd been under more stress than I'd thought.

Friday night, Joan and Marva came by. Joan brought me more homework and a large plastic star that caught the light like a prism to hang by my window. Marva brought a batch of health bars she'd made to help me get my strength back.

"I didn't know you'd made so many new friends," said my mother after they left.

"We all hang out together," I said. I helped myself to one of Marva's cookies. "I don't suppose you noticed that Joan and Marva are pretty odd too?"

"Odd?" repeated my mother. "What's odd about them?"

"You didn't notice that Joan dresses like it's 1953?" I asked.

My mother shrugged. "I thought it was the style," said my mother. "I thought she looked very nice."

"You didn't notice that Marva was wearing combat boots and a purple scarf with black bats stencilled on it?" I took another cookie. They weren't bad, even if they did have wheat germ and stuff like that in them.

"She could be a model," said my mother. "With those cheekbones." She gave me a look. "It's nice to see you eating again," she said.

On Saturday Chris showed up, carrying the telescope. I was in the kitchen having breakfast when my mother looked out the window over the sink and said, "Jenny, do you know a very good-looking boy who wears his hair in a pony-tail?"

I almost said no. I'd never heard anyone describe Chris as good-looking before. Weird, strange, brainy, crazy … but not good-looking. I thought about it. He was sort of good-looking. "Maybe," I said.

"He's carrying a telescope," said my mother.

I concentrated on wiping the syrup off the neck of the bottle. "It's Chris County, Marva's brother."

My Father invited him to join us. My mother asked if he was the boy with the owl. My father, immediately deciding that he'd found another bird fanatic, started talking about eagles. Chris knew as much about eagles as my father. The two of them were over the moon. My mother suggested that we set up the telescope in the attic, where there weren't any trees to block the way. My father asked Chris if he'd give him a hand with the storm windows. My mother asked Chris to stay to lunch. My father asked him if he'd seen the show on hoatzins a few weeks ago. They talked about hoatzins through the entire meal.

After Chris left, my father said, "Now that's what I call a nice young man."

I said, "You do? You don't think he's weird?"

"Weird how?" asked my mother.

Saturday afternoon, my mother ran into Amy in town. "She didn't realize you'd been sick," said my mother.

I didn't move my eyes from the book I was reading. I'd been home for four days, and Amy Ford hadn't noticed. I wasn't surprised, and I wasn't even disappointed. I was almost relieved. "What else did she say?" I asked.

"She said she was shopping for her Hallowe'en costume," said my mother. "She's going to be a mermaid."

I bit into my apple.

"You didn't tell me you were going to a Hallowe'en party," said my mother.

I bit into my apple again. "I'm not."

And suddenly I understood that the reason I'd been feeling so good the past few days wasn't really because I was avoiding my problems. It was because I was relaxing and being myself, without worrying what Amy and her friends were going to think. I was never going to be blonde, or tall or thin. So who cared? Amy didn't care. Amy hadn't given me a thought all week. But Marva had. And Tanya had. And Joan, Sue and Maria had. And so had Chris. And they definitely didn't care how tall I was, or how thin – or even if my hair was green.

"Jenny," said my mother, "have you and Amy had some sort of fight?"

"No," I said, "not really. We've just sort of drifted apart."

In a crazy way, I guess my problems really had sorted themselves.

Public as a frog

"**I** can't go through with it," I said to Chris. It was Tuesday afternoon. We were playing cards in the living-room, pretending that tomorrow was just another day. "I just can't."

Marva, who was lying on the couch, pretending to be dead, said, "Rititnitit."

"Shut up, Marva," said Chris. Then he turned back to me. "Why not?"

"Why not?" I gave a hollow laugh. "Christopher, a recent survey of American teenagers has shown that nine out of ten would prefer not to make a public spectacle of themselves if they can possibly help it. Especially in front of everyone they know."

"Fair enough," said Chris. "Your turn."

We'd put a lot of time and effort into making my sign and my costume. These, and my formal letter of protest to Mr Herrera, were already in my locker, waiting for tomorrow. But Chris didn't point out any of that.

"Dressing up as a frog definitely counts as making a public spectacle of yourself," I went on.

"Right," said Chris. "So don't do it."

I knew what he was up to. By being reasonable, he was trying to make me feel so guilty that I'd insist on going through with the plan. "I'd like to do it," I continued, "I really would. I know it's the right thing to do, it's not that. But I just can't face it." I threw out a queen. "I'm very shy and insecure."

"I know you're shy," said Chris. "That's why I think you should forget the whole thing." He picked up my queen.

"Really?"

"Rummy," said Chris.

"What have you got to eat?" asked Marva.

I felt much better once I'd made my decision. Well, I would, wouldn't I? I did the supper dishes in a good mood. I did my homework with a smile on my face. I sat down happily to watch a documentary about parrots with my father. "This is going to be good," said my father.

The documentary about parrots was awful. I mean, it was good, but it was awful. It started out by showing how beautiful and intelligent parrots are. Then it showed how wild parrots are captured, badly treated, and how a lot of them die gruesome deaths before they get to the pet store. It reminded me of frogs, not that frogs are as cute as parrots, or as intelligent, or as rare, or can be taught to talk. I mean, you wouldn't want some frog sitting on your shoulder, taking a peanut out of your mouth. But it reminded me of frogs anyway.

"You see how much we take for granted without really thinking about it?" said my father.

"I have to go to bed," I said. "I have a big day tomorrow looking for the internal organs of pond life."

I dreamt about frogs. Frogs with wings and pointy beaks. Or maybe I dreamt about parrots. Parrots with bulgy eyes and white bellies.

I was in the jungle with Mr Herrera and my biology class. We were all wearing pith helmets and carrying what looked like butterfly nets. "Now remember, class," Mr Herrera kept saying, "don't be squeamish. This is for science."

We ran through the jungle, shouting and yelling and scooping up frogs with our nets. Amy appeared in a clearing with Kim and Amber. They were in their Red Bay cheerleader's uniforms: red shorts, white blouses and red and white pompoms. They were jumping up and down and chanting. "If you're not with us, you miss the bus!" they boomed.

Amy started shaking her pompoms at me. "Jenny!" she called. "Jenny, watch! This one's for you!" She turned to Amber and Kim. "Ready, girls?" she smiled. They nodded. They spun to the left. They spun to the right. They did a split. "Do what you're told!" they all screamed. "Or end up in the cold!"

"Jenny!" Mr Herrera started shouting. "Jenny! Pay attention! You're letting the frogs get away!"

I looked around. I was up in a tree. Frogs were flying past me by the dozen.

"Get them!" screamed Mr Herrera. "Get them!"

"I'm getting them!" I screamed back. "Don't worry, Mr Herrera, I'm getting them!"

The cheerleaders' pompoms rustled. "Do what you're told! Do what you're told!" they yelled. "Do what you're told, or be out in the cold!"

"I'm getting them!" I screamed again. "I'm getting them!" I swung my net with all my might.

I fell out of the tree.

I walked to school by myself on Wednesday. Slowly. I don't know if everyone is wishy-washy when it comes to making decisions, or if once they made up their minds that's it. But not me. I make up my mind, and then I change it. Then I make it up again and then I change it

177

again. Make up; change. Make up; change. Here it was, D-Day, only a few hours before biology, and all the way to school I kept thinking, maybe I shouldn't dissect the frog after all. Maybe I should go through with the plan.

As I got to school, I saw Amy, Kim and Amber getting out of Kim's mother's car. They were talking and laughing. I got ready to smile, in case they turned round and saw me. Amy turned round. I smiled. She didn't see me. I stopped smiling and went back to being indecisive.

All through English and Spanish I wondered what I should do. Yes or no? ¿Sí o quizás? I decided to just walk by my locker on my way from Spanish to biology.

I walked past my locker. I stopped in front of my locker. I opened it. I took out the bag with the costume, the sign and the letter in it. I put it back again. I took it out. I pictured making that first incision in the frog's white belly. I imagined its tiny stomach and pancreas and heart. I smelled the formaldehyde. I raced into the girls' room and put my costume on.

Call me lucky, but even though I'd dithered, I got to the science building in plenty of time. There were only a few people in our classroom, and Mr Herrera was no-where in sight. He was probably getting the bodies out of the vault. Other kids were looking at me as you would look at someone wearing a lot of green papier-mâché, but

I ignored them. I stood in front of Mr Herrera's room for a few seconds, listening to my heart pound and wondering if I was going to stop breathing or not. I thought I might be paralysed, I was so scared. *What are you doing?* I was screaming to myself. *You are really out of your mind.* A few people laughed as they passed by.

"Who *is* that?" I heard someone ask.

"It's Jenny Kaliski," someone answered.

And that's when I thought, *Well, it's too late now. You're in the water now, you might as well swim.*

I hefted the sign against my shoulder. I took a deep breath. And I began to walk back and forth in front of the biology room. *One, two, three, turn*, I counted to myself. *One, two, three, turn.* There were unmistakable sounds of chairs being pushed back in a hurry and high school students rushing to see a fellow classmate make a complete fool of herself. There was more laughter. A crowd began to gather. If ever a person wanted to be astrally projected outside of her body, I was that person and the time was now. The only reason I kept going was because I couldn't stop.

And then I saw her. Out of the corner of my eye, I saw Amy standing on the other side of the hall with Kim and Rosie Henley. This time Amy saw me. I could tell from the look on her face that she saw me. It was the look of someone who's just discovered a bug swimming around in her cereal. She was shocked. She was disgusted. She was embarrassed. Boy, was she embarrassed! But more than that, I could tell she was mad. Mad at me. She'd dumped me, humiliated me, ignored me and hurt me – and now she was mad. *Do as you're told, or be out in the cold.* And suddenly I realized that the difference between me and Amy wasn't that she was taller and thinner and blonder than I would ever be. The difference was that she cared what people like Rosie Henley thought and I didn't. Why should I? In three years, we'd all be out of high school. Who would notice then if I'd hung out with the popular crowd or with the Martians? No one. Not Amy. Not Rosie Henley. Not me. And who would care if I'd stood up for the frogs of the world or not? I would.

"Miss Kaliski!" Mr Herrera was shouting. "Miss Kaliski, what is the meaning of this?"

I hadn't seen him sneaking up on me. I shook my sign. I gave him my biggest smile. "I'm peacefully protesting the meaningless dissection of frogs in your biology class," I said. My voice wasn't even shaking; it sounded strong and calm. I handed him my letter. "Here," I said, "this will explain everything."

As Mr Herrera reached for the envelope, there was a sudden explosion of light. We both turned.

"Mr County!" roared Mr Herrera. "I should have known you'd have a hand in this."

I blinked. There was Chris, grinning, with a camera in his hand. And right beside him were the Martians. They were grinning, too, and holding a banner that said SAVE THE FROGS!

"You didn't really think we'd let you do this by yourself, did you?" asked Chris.

He stayed with me all during third period while I was boycotting biology.

"You know," he whispered as we stood side by side against the wall, the sign resting between us, "Marva's thinking of having a Hallowe'en party this year."

"Well, I've already got my costume," I whispered back.

"And how about a date?" asked Chris.

I looked at him. "What?"

"A date," he repeated. "You don't already have that, do you?"

Kissing in the hallways of Red Bay High is against the rules. I think we might have done it anyway, but we were already in so much trouble.

The only thing Gabriela and
Beth have in common is that they
are in LA for the weekend. Gabriela
is there for FRIVOLITY, FASHION and
FUN; Beth for LECTURES, LEARNING and
LITERATURE. But what neither girl
knows is that they are not alone.
Two ANGELS are in LA with them.

AND THE ANGELS HAVE
OTHER IDEAS…

DYAN SHELDON

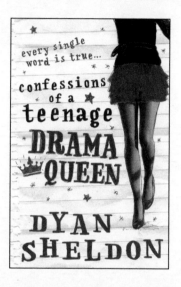

Everything I'm about to tell you
occurred exactly as I say — even
the things that seem so incredible,
so totally out of the solar system
that you think I must have made them
up. And nothing's been exaggerated,
not the teensiest, tiniest, most
subatomic bit. It all happened
exactly as I'm telling it.

And it starts with the end
of the world...

DYAN SHELDON

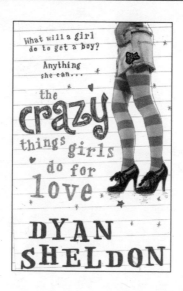

THREE very different girls
with one thing in common.

They all have a CRUSH on the
GORGEOUS NEW BOY in school.

But which of them will get him?
And how on earth is she going to
do it?

ALL IS FAIR IN LOVE AND WAR —
AND THIS IS LOVE!

DYAN SHELDON

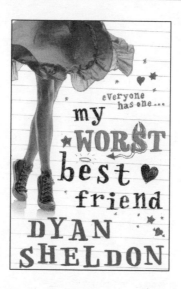

"Promise me you'll always be my best friend, Gracie," said Savanna. "No matter what happens. PROMISE. PROMISE. PROMISE." I laughed. "Of course I will," I promised.

It was a no-brainer. There was nothing that could ever end our friendship. We were SOUL SISTERS. We were COSMIC TWINS and we would be FOREVER.

AT LEAST THAT'S WHAT I THOUGHT THEN...

DYAN SHELDON